Crazy Jack

Crazy Jack

DONNA JO NAPOLI

Published by
Dell Laurel-Leaf
an imprint of
Random House Children's Books
a division of Random House, Inc.
1540 Broadway
New York, New York 10036

Visit us on the Web! www.randomhouse.com/teens

Educators and librarians, for a variety of teaching tools, visit us at www.randomhouse.com/teachers

ISBN: 0-440-22788-7

RL: 5.1

Reprinted by arrangement with Delacorte Press

Printed in the United States of America

August 2001

10 9 8 7 6 5 4 3 2 1

OPM

For Barry, who always
stands by his crazy woman

ACKNOWLEDGMENTS

Thanks to my whole family and to Diana Capriotti, Sheila Glasbey, Noëlle Paffett-Lugassy, Fiona Simpson, Stephanie Strassel, Richard Tchen, Jennifer Weiss, and Jennifer Wingertzahn. Thanks also to the many librarians at Swarthmore College and to Sharon Ford at Swarthmore's public library, all of whom helped me track down details of daily life in north-central England in the early 1500s.

But most of all, thanks go to Wendy Lamb for guiding me with patience and persistence.

CHAPTER ONE

The Farmer

Father sets a seed bag at the start of my row. "Go easy. Make the bag last the whole furrow."

"I will."

He smiles. "You know how almost as well as I do." He takes another seed bag, balances it on his shoulder, and walks bent as he plants. His hands squeeze the cut corner of the bag; seeds pour in a thin, steady stream. Other farmers carry only a half bag worth of seeds in baskets slung from their necks; no one works as hard as Father.

I cup my hands together. When Father first taught me

how to make a funnel of my palms, I was only four and his hands were huge around mine.

I'm nine now. I know how to scoop into the bag without spilling, then walk the row, watching a yellow ribbon of seeds fall from my hands onto the black dirt, soft from yesterday's rain. I know how to run back to the bag at the head of the row, waving my arms and shouting to scare off the birds till Father covers the seeds with the harrow.

The smells mix: heady soil, sweet grain. A worm wiggles by, grazing my big toe. There's not a crow or dove in the predawn glow—nothing to try to steal these seeds. The whole world encourages me. I heave the bag with all my might onto my shoulder, pucker the opening between my hands like Father, and bend. I walk the row, pouring seeds. At first they come too thick, but I tighten my hands just a little and they come perfectly. The work goes faster this way. As the heavy bag lightens, I'm practically running.

Father stands at the end of the row. His eyes size me up. "Good lad. You can finish this field by yourself. I'll go plant the south field."

I grin and run to pick up another bag.

It takes all morning to put in the wheat. But that's nothing compared to how long it took to prepare the fields for planting. Father and I have been working side by side for a week.

Father returns when I'm ready to start the last furrow. He guides the harrow that drags behind the mare, finishing the entire field just a quarter hour behind me. We walk together to the barn and release the mare. "You're a fine farmer, Jack. You work like a man."

I stand as tall as I can.

He smiles. "Still, you're not too big for a ride." Father winks and turns his back to me, crouching.

I touch the permanent stain on his right shoulder, the one left by seed bags. I climb on, my hands circling his forehead.

Father runs, holding me at the shins, and I soar, arms out to each side, fingers separated like the tips of a hawk wing.

Mother shades her eyes against the sun as we come up to the house. "Finished already?" The smell of peas-potage clings to her apron.

"Jack planted the wheat by himself, with a seed bag on his shoulder."

"The whole field?" asks Mother.

"Father did one row," I say.

"You're small for your age, Jack. Seed bags are heavy." Mother shakes her head, but a smile bursts forth. "Small but strong."

"He's my partner." Father swings me off his shoulders and I leap to the ground. He looks up at the clear sky. "It'll be a good harvest this year, I wager."

"We've had enough wagers, John."

Father gathers Mother into his arms. "This harvest needs no luck."

Last summer an oat blight hit. That's why we planted one field with wheat this year—if a blight hits, whether wheat or oat, we'll still have one field to harvest. Last year's blight left us nothing. So Father did wage labor at manors when he could find it and odd jobs in town, helping the rat catcher or raking the streets after market time.

But most of all he made wagers. He never told me what the wagers were about. He said, "There's things a boy shouldn't be part of." I know some of it was wrestling; he's the strongest wrestler around. He came home with wonderful things—a skinning knife for me or a bolt of cloth for Mother or a slab of bacon for himself.

Mother turned everything to good use. She cleaned the skin of the coneys I snared and sold them to the furrier. She sewed nightslips for babies and sold them in town. She took half of Father's bacon and put it in country pies with egg and onion to trade for whatever she could.

The pies stopped when Father lost our chickens. Father can be unlucky now and then. Anybody can. But he's mostly lucky. Someday he's going to win us some sheep.

I like sheep, their funny wide-set eyes and how they bleat. Last month I worked for the Hedley clan through shearing time, picking bits of leaves and sticks from the lye-soaked fleece. I brought home a hard round ball of sheep cheese for Father and a half dozen skeins of wool yarn for Mother. They were so pleased, they laughed. Not much feels better than that.

I reach into my pocket. "Look, Mother." In the center of my palm is a clump of seeds that were matted together in the bottom of one bag. "See? They look like a lamb."

Mother nods. "You've got a good imagination, Jack."

"Do you want help in your flower garden?" asks Father.

Mother's eyes light up. "I suppose the midday meal can wait." She twirls around and goes into the barn, coming out with a shovel and two trowels. We march to her garden. Beyond it, across our field, stands Flora's house. I wave, just in case she's watching.

"All this?" Father looks across the wide area, surprised.

"Flowers for sale," Mother calls in her flowermonger's lilt. Last autumn, when we had no harvest to bring to market, Mother sold her chrysanthemums in town.

Father gives a half smile. "This year, Meg, we'll be selling grain at the August fair all week long."

"Don't I know that? But flowers can't hurt. And the townsfolk deserve a little country pleasure, too." Mother looks Father full in the face.

I love it when her face opens like that. Mother is as beautiful as Flora, though they don't look anything alike, Mother fair and Flora rich brown. Mother hands Father the shovel and shows him clusters of shoots to separate and transplant. I weed. Like Father said, I'm a fine farmer.

After a while, my stomach growls.

Mother's beside me on her hands and knees, digging with her trowel. She sits back on her heels and looks at me. "We're done here for today. And I was thinking this much work would take me all afternoon." She stands up. "I don't suppose you two would like bread and cheese for a late meal beside the swimming hole."

Father knocks a clod of dirt off his shovel with his heel. "It's a good time for fishing, after a rain."

"That's what I was thinking." I jump to my feet and hand Mother my trowel. "Can I fetch Flora?"

Mother twists her mouth. "Beth needs her more each day."

5

Beth is Flora's mother and she's pregnant. Again. But she's unlucky. The only child she's carried to term is Flora. Mother says she should have stopped trying long ago. Mother stopped trying after me.

"If Flora comes, I can help with her work later. I can scrape the milk pails clean. And I'm good at churning. Let me go ask, Mother. At least let me ask."

Mother puts her fingertips to her lips. "Don't you have work to do for your father later?"

I'm supposed to scour the open countryside for wild feverfew plants. We set them growing here and there in the fields and they keep out the insects. I look at Father. "I can work extra fast the rest of the week. I'll make up for an afternoon off. You know I will."

Father hands Mother his shovel. "Pack the food. I'll go with Jack to get Flora." He walks into the house and comes out holding his tambourine drum.

I'm grinning now as I run ahead, flying with the drumbeat across the grasses and through the opening of the whitewashed wall around Flora's home.

She comes out of the henhouse with a wire basket over her arm. Brown eggs line the bottom.

"Come fishing with us."

"Fishing?" Flora's eyes light on Father, who's already walking around to the back shed where her father makes cheese. "Is he going to ask Papa?"

"Yep. Look." I hold out the clump of wheat seeds.

Flora puts down the basket. "Is it a cat? No, not with that tiny tail. Hmmm." She knits her brows. Then her face goes soft. "A lamb."

6   "Right. For you."

Flora takes the clump and sets it carefully on the window ledge.

Father comes out of the shed, his shirt smelling of sharp cheddar.

Flora picks up the egg basket and holds it against her chest, both arms wrapped around it. "Did Papa put you to work?"

"Yep," says Father. "I tightened the presses. And I promised Jack would do chores with you later."

Flora's eyes smile. "And was that enough for him to let me go?"

"Nope."

Her face falls.

"He wants the first five fish we catch, too." Father laughs.

Flora hums and just about dances as she goes into the house to leave the eggs.

I know how she feels. I'm dancing and dancing to Father's drum.

CHAPTER TWO

August

"Don't bother him, Jack." Mother catches me by the arm as I'm halfway through the door.

Father's been standing at the edge of the south field for a long time. His sweat-soaked shirt sticks to his back. "I won't, Mother. I won't even talk. I'll just stand by him."

"All right."

"Wait." Flora's mother gets up from the kitchen table, where she's been fingering the baby nightslips. She takes her straw hat from the peg by the door and puts it on my head. "Don't get sunstroke out there."

"What's sunstroke?"

She smiles. "My father-in-law warned me that strong sun can knock you over."

Her father-in-law. That's Flora's grandfather. He was a servant to rich people before he came here from Spain, where the sun shines hot. This amazing heat must be what it's like there all the time.

Flora's mother sits again. "I'll buy some of those night-slips, but I want to order special ones, too."

Mother flushes. "Don't buy what you don't need, Beth. You're on hard times, too."

"Cheese makers aren't hurting as bad as farmers. And my eyes haven't been so good lately." Flora's mother lowers her voice, as though she's confiding. "The astrologist says it's 'cause I'm carrying a boy. I eat boiled hedgehog fat, but it doesn't seem to help much. Otherwise I'd sew nightslips myself. I can't even crochet a blanket."

"I can crochet a blanket."

"Would you?"

"I'd be happy to. It'll be my gift to that strong son inside you. After all, we'll be family when Flora and Jack are grown."

They're not watching me, so I quietly hang the hat back up and lope out the door. Flora's mother needs her hat specially, since she's with child. Just a few feet from Father, I slow to a walk. The heat wraps around my arms and face, alive.

Father doesn't say a word, but he walks with me along one side of the field, then along the side where the south field meets the east field. "Nothing's green," he says. "No color."

The wheat we planted three months ago came up. The oats came up. But the rain the day before we planted was the last rain we've had. When the little shoots came up, they barely got a chance to leaf out before they withered. Father and Mother and I all carried buckets of water from the well. Buckets of water from the swimming hole. But we couldn't beat the sun.

I can barely stand to look at the lifeless stalks. Mother's garden is brown, too. A dry spell doesn't care about the difference between wheat and oats. It doesn't care what's a flower.

"Jack? There just might be enough time to do another seeding."

"What will seeds do in dry soil?"

"The soil can't stay dry forever." Father scratches his chest. "The trick is to get the seeds in the earth either just after a rain or just before one."

That sounds right—that's the trick. And Father can be tricky.

"Some farmers already put in a second planting. They're losing a second time. But I waited, Jack. I waited."

I nod. "You were smart."

"I can't wait any longer, though. Autumn will come when it comes. We have to take a chance."

"I'm your partner. I'm ready."

"I knew you would be." Father sticks his bottom lip out and blows so that the air goes up his face.

I do the same. It's almost cooling.

"Seed is hard to come by now. I'll have to make a

wager if I want to get it. And the stakes will have to be high. I'll have to offer something important."

I don't look at him. "What will you offer?"

"The wagon."

The wagon. How will we carry harvest to market without the wagon? Every farmer needs a wagon. "Does Mother know?"

"Nope. Now go sit in the shade. We'll work hard as soon as I get back." Father goes to the barn.

I stand and watch him drive off with the wagon, my bottom lip out, huffing and puffing to cool my face.

• • •

At noon, Mother and I eat bread and onions. Father's been gone for hours. I chew extra long out of nervousness. I wash it all down with cider. This is the end of last year's cider, and it's hard now, fizzy and sour like ale.

I'm feeling almost woozy when Father finally appears. Oh, thank you, Lord—he's driving the wagon.

"Hey!" I call from the window, waving like a madman. I strip off my shirt and run out to him. "Let's plant!"

Father laughs. "We'll plow first, Jack. And we'll plant every last seed. Then we'll build a system of ditches to carry water to the plants, like the Romans built just about everywhere but here." He hoists a bag of seed over one shoulder, then adds a second one. He lets out a long whistle. "Sometimes you've got to take a risk."

I pick up a seed bag and carry it to the barn. "We'll have everything we need again."

"Food on the table, a roof over our heads, and each other. That's all we need, boy."

"Maybe you can buy back the chickens," I say.

"Maybe. And maybe that flock of sheep you're always asking for."

We're both laughing now.

CHAPTER THREE

Getting There

"Jack."

I wake to Father shaking me by the shoulder.

"I'm going to town. Meet me outside the wheelwright's at noon. You hear me?"

"Yes, sir."

"Now go back to sleep."

I fall onto my straw mat and shut my eyes. Today the August fair begins. My skin tingles. The first day of the fair is the best day of the season, and since the August fair is the best fair, this is the best day of the year.

Or it should be.

But it still hasn't rained. The creek dried up and the swimming hole kept shrinking, so there was no water to fill the ditches Father and I dug. Most of our second planting didn't even start to grow and what did, shriveled up and blew away.

All the farmers are scrambling for extra work, but there isn't enough to go around. Father hasn't found odd jobs. And no one gives a job to a boy like me.

Still, Father has won wagers.

And I've gotten good at finding wild parsnips in the countryside. They're short and gnarly from lack of rain, but they're something to put on the table.

I can hear Mother's snore through the wall. She stayed up late last night, sewing by candlelight.

"Jack. Jack, wake up," Flora calls.

I climb out the window and drop in the dirt beside her. Dawn spreads soft everywhere.

"Why'd you stay in bed so late? We'll miss things." She smells like sleep.

"You just woke up, too, Flora." I give her hair a playful yank.

She ducks away. "Let's go."

We cross the dry field at a run. Nothing's about at this hour except sheep grazing on yellow grasses far off and coneys that are so busy foraging, they don't even hop away as we pass. We scrabble over Flora's wall, side by side, into the midst of the pecking chickens.

I miss the taste of chicken. But we still have two young hogs. If we can only feed them enough to make them grow, by next winter we'll have chops and sausage and shoulder boiled with cabbage. And Father'll eat bacon again. He loves his bacon.

Flora pinches me. "You promised you'd be here before the sun."

"I lay in bed. But I didn't move about for fear of waking Mother." I pick up a pebble and clean it on my shirt. "She was up late."

"Oh."

I spit on the pebble and rub it harder. It's nice and smooth. I drop it in Flora's hand.

She rolls it between her palms. "Hurry, before Papa leaves." She ducks down at the corner of her house to drop my pebble into her tin box and runs on.

"Jack." Flora's mother leans from the window. She holds out a bundle wrapped in a kerchief. "Put a little something in that stomach." Her own stomach is huge with child now. But her face is lean. Yesterday I watched her stroking the milk cows, running both hands across their ribs. We're all getting thin.

"Thank you." I take the bundle, hot in my hands. An egg, of course—she knows I miss eggs—but there's something else, too. I smile up at her. Then at Flora.

Flora and I are exactly the same size, the same age. We've known each other all our lives. We stood behind her woodpile and pledged to marry each other years ago.

I boost Flora into the back of the wagon, and she pulls me up. The wagon lurches down the lane to the main road.

Flora's father looks over his shoulder at us, holding the reins taut. "If robbers should think of attacking, they'll think twice." He rubs the hunting bow that lies across his lap.

"My father says no one's been robbed on this road for months now, because of the reward." The biggest families, the clans, will give a handsome purse to anyone who catches or kills a robber.

"True enough. But the longer they go without robbing, the more likely it is that they won't be able to hold out any longer."

I wish I had my skinning knife on me. "I'll help if they attack."

Flora hands me a stone from her pocket. "One for you, one for me. We can throw stones at them. At the giant, too." Her words are brave, but her face speaks the truth, as always: she's afraid.

I take a quick look at Flora's father, but he's busy driving. He didn't hear her. People say the giant can run by, tuck a sheep under each arm, and keep on running. They say he's taken women, too. "The giant plagues the valley on the other side of the great cliff," I say. "He's never been seen in these parts, Flora." Still, I move slightly in front of her. I'm strong, after all.

Flora holds her stone with both hands and stares out her side of the wagon.

We ride in silence past thick forests of king's oak and holm oak and Scots pine and a few scattered beech. The calm of the woods gradually enters me. "No one's going to attack this morning."

Now I remember to open the kerchief Flora's mother gave me: a hard-cooked egg and a muffin.

Flora looks at me and smiles.

"Have a bite," I say, though I want every crumb.

"I already ate." She laughs as I gobble the muffin. Then she says, "Help me."

We work together, shoving the heaviest rounds of cheese to make a place to nestle in, the back of her head hard on my chest, her feet next to mine, so that it seems as if I have four feet. This is how we travel when we go to market in her father's wagon. We watch the clouds in the brightening sky. Flora hums. I eat the egg slowly, making each bite last. In one hand, my egg; in the other, my stone. Ready.

"The new baby will love cheese." Flora runs one hand along the leaves that coat a cheese wheel. Her fingers play with a loose dock leaf.

"Next year we can take him to the fair with us," I say.

"He'll love the animal exchange. Especially the birds." Flora laughs again. She loves all animals, but birds are her favorite. She can identify them by song or sight. Her hands now make happy chickadees in the air over her chest. "Papa thinks he can sell all these cheeses during fair week. If he does, you know what he promised to get me?"

"A *palacio* like the one your grandfather lived in."

"Make a real guess."

But my mind doesn't want to think about real things. I can see the house in my head. All the houses in this part of England are mud and timber—but the house Flora should live in is the stone house in my head, surrounded by the groves and groves of orange trees that Flora's grandfather told us about. "We'll go to Spain one day, Flora."

"I don't want to. They kill bulls as a game there."
Flora sits up and faces me. "Guess or I'll have to tell
you."

"Tell me."

"A new dress for the baby's baptism."

"A store-bought dress?"

"I'm going into the dress shop today to look around."

I've never had a store-bought shirt or britches. I don't
have to look down to know my legs stick out way past the
bottom of my trousers. Mother could make me a new pair
if she wasn't so tired at night. She's been taking in sewing
for others since the crops failed.

Drought. I'd never heard that word until a couple of
months ago. The farmers around here are baffled; their
fathers and their grandfathers didn't face drought. Something's very wrong here. Someone must have crossed a
fairy.

Everyone knows a fairy won't abide being spoken of.
People say that someone must have told of a fairy favor
and now we're all being punished. Fairies control the
power of the sun. Too much sun and everything dries out,
loses its color. Yes, we're under a fairy spell.

I stare at the light blue sky, such a comforting color.
"D'you think it'll ever rain, Flora?"

"It has to."

I know that. If it doesn't rain eventually, we won't be
able to go on. That's what I heard Mother whisper to
Father one night.

Flora snakes her arm through mine. "It'll rain and then
shine—and the whole world will be rainbows. Don't
think about it now. The fair opens today."

The road fills with wagons and oxcarts and people on foot. Now meadows and pastures stretch out yellow and quiet on both sides. Dodd castle rises to the north. The wagon swerves hard to the right. I grab the stone and rise to my knees to see what's up, Flora at my shoulder. A monk on horseback approaches. It's bad luck to meet clergy on the road. That's why Flora's father turned the wagon; he's careful to let the monk pass on our left, the only thing that can shield us from the harm. Cold fear makes my teeth hurt.

The monk wears sleeves even in this heat. They are garnished at the hand. A wrought gold pin fastens his hood, yet I see his fat cheeks.

Flora's father shakes his head. "They own too much land," he says over his shoulder to me.

Father doesn't like them, either. He says they have so much money that they don't even feel the effects of this drought. But we have to be grateful for the monk. We have to be grateful for the men who live in manor houses or castles, for without working their lands a summer ago, how would Father have fed us through last winter?

And who cares if they're rich? Like Flora says, someday it will rain again and we'll plant and have plenty of food. Life will be good for all of us, like it used to be.

"Oh, look, Jack." Flora points ahead to the stalls that have sprung up at the edge of town. The marketplace in the town center must be overflowing.

Flora's father steers the wagon off the road and pulls to a halt. "Help me set up."

We arrange the cheese at the edge of the wagon closest to the road. First the medium-sized ones—the cloves—

weighing seven pounds each. Behind them we stack the huge pondus; each one weighs six cloves. Most of these cheeses are aged, from last spring and winter, for the cows haven't been giving as much milk this summer.

The man who sells smoked ham sides is crossing the road to see what's in the wagon. I half remember the taste of ham. It's even better than the smell.

"All right," says Flora's father. "Go enjoy the fair."

CHAPTER FOUR

The Fair

Flora takes my hand and we hurry along the road into town. "Look, a monkey." He wears a hat and holds a tin cup for coins. She puts out her hand and the monkey grabs her finger.

"Leave him alone." The owner scoops the monkey into his arms and glowers at Flora. "Go on."

Flora stiffens.

The man flicks the back of his hand at us. "Foreigners."

"I was born in England," says Flora. "I'm as English as you."

"You don't fool me, little vagrant."

I put my arm around Flora's waist and force her away with me.

"My papa has more cows than you'll ever dream of," Flora shouts over her shoulder.

"Shhh. You don't sound English when you say things like 'papa.'" I push her past the wool brogger, the ropemaker, the maltster, thinking how true her words are. We have three cows; Flora's family has two dozen. Her father has done well for himself, even if people don't trust a Spaniard. If it weren't for the drought, Flora's family would be rich. "Forget him."

"But he called me a vagrant. Vagrants get whipped."

"He's hardly more than a vagrant himself."

Rows of stalls fill the main market square, and the special court is already set up with the official weights and measures.

"Let's head for the livestock first," says Flora.

We run past the leather from Coventry, the stockings from Nottingham, the hats from all the way down in Bedford. There's no end of Mendip lead, Cornish tin, Tyneside coal.

Now we race down the aisle of grain stalls. I look at the mounds of oats brought in by boat along the Tyne from Newcastle and the barley brought in from Carlisle. Why do they have rain but not a drop for our part of the uplands?

22 Father grew barley one year. I remember, because

Mother brewed beer from it. The vapors from the steaming malt would have drugged Mother to sleep but for the fact that I kept singing and telling jokes and dancing around so that she laughed the whole time. And I'm the one who gathered the wild germander, to make the beer dark and flavorful. Everyone liked that beer, and Father traded it for whatever we wanted. He got me apples all fall and winter.

I lift my nose to see if I can smell apples in the market. Most of the fruits and vegetables are from Cumberland or Northumbria, and apples won't be ripe there for another couple of weeks. So I'm hoping for apples from the south, maybe from Wales. But Flora pulls me along toward the livestock. We pass the morning there, Flora singing to the geese and swans and peacocks.

But my hunger returns. "Come on. Let's find a fruitmonger." Fruitmongers usually need help carrying stock here and there, and they pay in fruit.

"Cherries, Jack. I want Scottish cherries."

We follow an aisle of the market stalls, alert for opportunities. There's a crowd ahead—people come away with meat on sticks. The smell of venison is so strong, I can taste it.

We push along with everyone else. I put my hand on the arm of the man in front of me. "How's a fellow to earn a meat stick?"

"It's free, lad. The lord of a manor has roasted up deer from his own deer park. Enough for everyone."

I grin. It feels like Christmas, when we carry our dishes and mugs to the manors for a feast.

But Flora shakes her head. "Nothing's free."

"And you're right, lassie," says a man who stands behind us now. "We're all paying. Every time those deer wander out through a hole in the wooden pale around the parks, they eat what our sheep and cattle need." The man lifts an eyebrow. "This lord is trading meat for our goodwill, he is."

A drummer walks by playing loudly, but not half as sprightly as Father. The noon bells ring. And, oh, I've got to get to the wheelwright's to meet Father. But I'm so close to the meat now, the smell is like to drive me crazy. And Father wouldn't want me to miss a free meal.

We press ahead.

"Look." Flora points at the dog tethered to a handle of the spit. The scullion slaps the dog's rump to keep him walking in a circle. "Poor thing."

The scullion is stripped naked because of the heat from the roasting fire. A man yells at him, and he leaves the dog and cuts more meat, skewering it for the crowd. I wonder if he's freeman or serf.

At last we're at the front. We take our meat and eat as we walk.

"Venison is good," I say.

"I prefer rabbit," says Flora.

"Call them coneys. When you say 'rabbit,' everyone thinks you're a foreigner."

"It's not how I talk, Jack. It's how I look. And I can't change that." She tosses her head. "I wouldn't even if I could."

"I'm glad."

24   She smiles at me, bold as anything.

At the corner we find the wheelwright's, but Father's not there.

"Maybe he was in a hurry and when you didn't show up at noon, he left." Flora licks meat juice off her fingers. "I'm going to look at dresses now. The shop's just over there. Come with me."

"I have to wait for Father."

"Please, Jack."

"I can't go in with you anyway."

"But you can wait for me outside." Her eyes hold me. She wants me near; she's afraid the clothier will think she's a vagrant.

"When Father comes we'll cross the street and wait for you at the shop door."

Flora hesitates, then straightens her smock. "All right." She doesn't look back.

She spends a long time in the shop. I look up and down the street. Where is Father?

At last Flora emerges and comes to me. "There's another shop two streets over." Her voice doesn't plead, but her eyes do.

If Father were coming, he'd have been here by now. "Let's go."

We pass through a street so narrow that the third floors of the houses nearly meet over our heads. Flora spends just as long inside the second shop. I don't care, though. I love being in town, watching the people pass. I walk to the busy thoroughfare, where a juggler stops and winks at me. He performs for a few moments—my private show. A woman passes with a birdcage balanced on her head. Flora would have wanted to see that. I visit the apothecary stall set up across the way and examine the huge stoneware jars of coriander and licorice and saffron and borage root. The strong smells make me hazy.

Flora comes out at last and skips ahead. "Let's go help Papa."

For the rest of the day I'm happy toting cheese home for buyers, happy in the wagon as we bump along toward home. I tell Flora all the things I saw when she was in the clothier's, every little detail of the woman with the birdcage. She laughs, like I knew she would.

A bow rests across my lap, just like the bow on Flora's father's lap. He borrowed my bow from a man in town when he heard of a robbery on the road from the north. I'll hold the bow like this as we travel in the wagon to and from the fair all week.

I sit tall, trying to look fierce. But it's hard, because Flora tickles me between feeding me bits of cheddar.

When we arrive at her home, Flora's father hands me a small round of cheese.

"I didn't earn it," I say in astonishment.

"Take it." He unharnesses the horses, all busy.

"I'll come early the rest of the week," I say. "I'll help with the horses. And at the end of the week, I'll scrub the wagon."

I walk home and place the cheese on the table in front of Mother.

She looks at the cheese with slow eyes. Then she stares at me. Tear streaks line her cheeks.

"What happened?"

She shakes her head. She looks so sad, I feel tears in my own eyes. When someone cries, there I go.

I come around the table and kneel beside her, putting my arms around her middle. She's sobbing now. My heart clutches. "Where's Father? What happened?"

Mother shakes her head.

I hug her tight. My head feels strange and light. "Tell me."

"Your father made a wager."

"That's nothing new."

"He wagered for a flock of sheep. What a farmer wants with sheep I don't know."

I feel queasy.

"He lost our fields, Jack. They belong to Ian Hedley now."

Our fields. Oh, Lord.

He lost everything.

CHAPTER FIVE

Weather

Mother and Father fight. They never used to, but for the past few weeks that's all I hear. I'm outside, under the window.

"What use is a field when there's no rain?" says Father, so sad.

And I think of Flora, as sad now as anyone. Flora's baby brother and mother died yesterday, the one right after the other.

Everyone's world is turning upside down, as though some colossal evil dragon juggles us all.

I press my back against the side of the house and slide down, wedged between my heels and the wall. Squeezed like this, morning hunger doesn't ache so much. Lucky Ben's orchard lies just a couple of miles down the lane. My imagination's in top form today or the wind's extra strong, because I'm sure I smell those pears. Can't be. I know it can't be; I helped pick the pitiful few that ripened a couple of weeks ago—a month early. My head knows that, but my nose breathes in the smell of phantom pears, thick-skinned and juicy.

But I can't leave in case Father and Mother need me. Ever since I let Father down on opening day at the fair— when I was too late at the wheelwright's—I've been careful to be reliable.

Maybe Father wouldn't have run off if I'd met him the way I was supposed to.

Or maybe Father never showed up himself. Maybe he ran off that morning right after the wager. I can't get up the nerve to ask him, though I want to know.

The rain comes, gentle at first.

Warm rain.

I won't believe it. Rain to soak the earth. Cruel rain.

Soon it pelts. The drops sting my cheeks. They grow cold and I shiver. Inside, they're shouting now. Does Mother know it's raining? Does she know the fields are already healing?

The gnawing in my stomach grows worse.

This fight is nothing special. It's got to be nothing special. Nothing new has happened—nothing big. It's only my imagination that heard something frightening in their voices—my brain working overmuch, as

Mother says. She can't get madder at him because of the rain.

I listen; maybe they're hugging each other. Sometimes after they fight, they cling to each other. Sometimes they gather me into their circle, too, all warm and safe.

Maybe they're calling for me. But the rain drums out everything except my hunger.

. . .

It hasn't stopped raining for two whole days. We sit at the table drinking milk hot from the cow. It feels so good.

Father puffs on his pipe. He won the tobacco in a wager with a smuggler. Mother called him reckless and told him to sell it—but he said he didn't dare risk the public whipping he'd get for selling smuggled goods. I think the real reason he keeps it is because he loves it. He seems almost happy after a pipe.

Mother wipes her hands on her apron now and leans over the basket by her feet. She takes out the ball of yarn, the crochet hook, the almost-finished blanket. She works quickly, silently. Last night she whispered, "Beth," as she worked—little bursts in the dark. But now she just rocks her head.

Flora's father gives his special knock on the door. I open it and he steps in and takes off his wet cap so that his hair sticks out in every direction. He nods to Father, to Mother.

Father stands up and nods back. "Have a seat, Gonzalo. Would you care for a pipe?"

The thin man shakes his head. "We'll be needing the blanket by midday."

Mother stands and spreads her arms, holding the blanket so that he can see it clearly. It's big enough to cover the mother and child easily, though the baby will be wrapped as well in the smaller blanket Mother made a month ago. The pattern is more intricate than anything I've ever seen her do before. She copied it from a shawl Flora's father showed her. "It'll be ready."

"You're a fast worker."

Mother doesn't say that she stayed up working in the dark, that she got up at dawn and worked. She gathers the blanket together and sits again, her hand twisting the hook faster and faster. Her cheeks go blotchy and I know she's holding back tears.

I think of Flora's mother tucking a stray lock of hair behind her ear as she smiled. She carried the clean scent of buttermilk with her everywhere. I swallow the lump in my throat.

"One large round of cheese, that's what we agreed upon," Flora's father says. "I'll bring it at midday."

"Why don't you keep that cheese for now?" says Mother. "You gave us a round last month."

"That was small."

"And delicious. When we need more, I'll tell you."

What is she saying? We make cheese, sure—but barely enough to feed the three of us now that the cows are so skinny. It's nowhere near as good as the cheese Flora's father makes, anyway. And we could trade his cheese for flour and eggs.

Flora's father looks from Mother to Father, but Father tapped out his pipe and now he's fooling with his clog. "All right," the little man says. "You tell me when." He leaves.

"You planning on worse times ahead?" asks Father.

"Gonzalo's hurting, spending so much." Mother presses the back of her hand to her nose. "And when he was expecting joy instead of grief."

It's true: a funeral costs more than a wedding, more than a baptism. The priest took the second-best cow Flora's Father had. And the funeral food must be good—a hotchpotch of meats and herbs, roasted capons and pigeons and pheasants, venison with jelly.

I wince: Mother did right to turn down the cheese. It's hunger that scrambled Father's and my thoughts.

Father looks briefly at me. Then he walks to the window and throws the shutters open to the rain.

"Close those shutters," says Mother. "There's no point getting wet before you have to."

Father dug the double grave yesterday afternoon and we spread his clothes out by the fire overnight. He'll fill in the dirt after they're buried today, and he'll get soaked to the bone again.

Two chickens he'll get for his labors. Two. My mouth waters. Father won't tell Flora's father to wait before giving us the two, because he knows Flora's family can get more chickens just by letting a couple of eggs sit till they hatch. So taking the chickens can't be wrong. Yesterday afternoon Father put his arm around my shoulder and told me he was looking forward to filling my belly with a good meal. "We'll eat chicken at noon," I say, to make Father smile.

"We'll eat plenty at the wake this afternoon," says Mother. "No need to cook our own meal first."

"Then chicken tomorrow noon." I smile at Father.

"Eggs," says Mother. "Eggs are . . ."

"We'll eat chicken tomorrow noon," says Father. "You heard the lad. I don't disappoint my own son."

Mother jerks her head toward him, but she doesn't speak. Father hears her silence, too.

I want to say something to make things right, but there's nothing to say.

Mother turns to me. "Jack, you want a big chicken feast on the morrow, or you want eggs often? It's raining now—the earth will pump out chicken feed, like it used to. We can keep those chickens alive easy on the land around the house. We can have eggs with our bread and onions." She's talking fast. "I asked for a rooster and a hen. We can start a little chicken yard again. Within six months, we can be eating chicken once a week."

"We'll eat chicken tomorrow noon," says Father. "Just like a lord in a manor house."

. . .

I sit on the back stoop of Flora's house with a bowl of pudding, trying to stay out of the way, my legs tucked under me so they won't stick out in the drizzle. The house is crowded with noisy grown-ups.

Flora comes and sits beside me. She takes my hand, opens her fist, and pours in a small pile of sugar lumps.

I gape. I've never tasted sugar before, but I recognize it, because I've seen candy made at the fairs. This sugar was supposed to be for the baptismal celebration.

"What's that you gave the lad?" The baker Evelyn leans out the door.

My hand darts under the hem of my shirt.

"Just crumbs," says Flora.

I don't know where she gets the gumption to lie.

"Looked like sugar lumps to me. Looked like what the guests will want to suck on once they've finished with the honey cakes. Sugar's expensive."

"It came from Spain," says Flora softly.

"If the guests can't suck on sugar, they'll be grousing for more cakes."

"There's plenty of cakes," says Flora. "Good cakes. And plenty of sugar lumps, too." Flora turns the back of her head to the baker Evelyn and stares out at nothing. I've never turned my head away from an adult who was speaking to me. Never.

The baker Evelyn disappears inside.

"Thank you," I whisper.

Flora looks over her shoulder to the door. She sticks out her tongue. She smiles at me.

I'm not fooled. "I'm sorry your mother died. And your baby brother."

"So am I, Jack." She hums. But she's got the saddest face I've ever seen.

· · ·

Early the next morning the rain stops. The scent makes me feel new and strong.

"Breakfast, Jack." Mother puts two fried eggs on my plate.

I know what she's doing. The hen laid two eggs—and Mother's giving both to me so I'll side with her against Father about killing it for the noon meal.

Mother puts a basket of hot soda biscuits on the table. I don't stop to breathe till I've finished.

34 "Jack, you want eggs again tomorrow? Why don't you

fix up that old chicken coop and help me get a brood going?"

I look at Father, asleep on his back where he dropped when we got home last night. Mother and I were so tired, we just left him there. He got drunk at the wake and he'll be sick today. I pick up the plate and lick it. "All right."

"I wish there was something for your father to do."

"Flora's father said he'd pay someone to carry a letter all the way to London and make sure it gets on a boat for Spain. It'll be good money."

Mother shakes her head. " 'Tis a sad world when a death brings more prosperity than our own daily work." She sighs.

"Death brings prosperity," comes Father's groggy voice as he rolls over in half sleep.

I go out the door to the old chicken coop. That's when I see it. The rainbow streaks from the west horizon to the top of the cliff on the east. The fairy spell is broken at last. I laugh to see that rainbow shimmer. I count the colors: six. No, seven: violet, indigo, blue, green, yellow, orange, red. It colors the whole world. I run along the lane, arms stretched high.

Flora was right.

CHAPTER SIX

Holes

I hear Mother shouting and I run home again.

Father's in the side yard with the axe in one hand and the rooster by the neck in the other. Mother's hanging on his axe arm, shouting. She's told me a thousand times never to get near someone swinging an axe. She's lost her head. Like the chicken will soon.

"Father, the rainbow," I shout. I'm in front of him now, so he can't swing that axe without killing me, too. I point. Something's got to stop him. "Please." Please put down the axe. Please, Father.

Father's mouth opens and his eyes shine as he looks up. He turns to Mother in a daze. "What's an honest man to do?" He drops the axe. His free hand wipes slowly across his mouth. "Our luck will improve. We'll sit down to a proper meal soon enough." He hands Mother the chicken and goes inside.

Mother sets the chicken on the ground. He runs off, his neck bent crazy to one side but his legs as strong as ever. His partner joins him, clucking like a demon. "Don't set yourself in front of an axe ever again, Jack. I have to put up with one fool. Don't make me put up with two."

"Yes, ma'am." I go inside.

Father's sitting at the table, his pipe in one hand, the box of smuggled tobacco in front of him. But he isn't stuffing the pipe. He's just sitting there. "Why'd you point at the rainbow?"

"I wanted you to see it."

"You know about the pot of gold?"

"Course I do. It's at the end of the rainbow."

Father smiles at me.

"Maybe I'll go to the end of the rainbow." My own words surprise me because I know that the pot at the end of the rainbow is so far no child could ever walk there. And this rainbow passes over the top of the cliff. Still, I'm trying my best to keep that smile on his face. "Maybe I'll get it for us. Then all our troubles will be over."

"Don't go thinking that you've got to solve our troubles. I do what needs doing."

"Course you do."

Father snaps the tobacco box shut. "If it's gold you   37

want, I'll get it, I will. There's ways. We can even be rich. You believe me, don't you, Jack?"

I think of Flora lying to the baker Evelyn. "Course I do."

. . .

By afternoon the rain's back. It's pouring and I'm in the barn looking at the hole in the thatched roof. I'm pretty sure I could fix it. When the sun comes out again, I'll give it a try.

The cows shift their weight from hoof to hoof. Three restless cows. They'd rather be out in the rain, but Mother told me to bring them in. Their sour grass smell hangs warm and dense about my head.

I climb up to the rickety loft and stick my head out the hole. Lightning flashes. Excitement jingles from my neck down my body. I've always loved a storm, and we've waited so long for this one. Lightning flashes and lights up the whole lane. I see Father walking there, coming home at a fast clip, his head bent into the wind, his shoulders hunched. He goes into the cottage. As he opens the door, I can see that his hands are empty. He was supposed to come home with a satchel of seeds so that Mother could plant a kitchen garden. We still own the land closest to the house, after all, the land where she had her flower garden. She's been wanting bean seeds most. And those new things that grow from eyes in their sides—potatoes, they're called. She's got to plant soon to have an autumn garden before winter sets in.

Lightning flashes. I'd better get inside now. But what's that? A rusty face low around the rear corner of the

cottage.

A fox. Out and about before dusk.

And I left the chickens running free. "Where are you?" I shout. The chickens strut not ten feet from the fox, picking at the mud. Idiots. "Go away, Fox! Go away!"

Father bursts out the door just as the fox makes a dash. A chicken in its mouth, and it's gone. Father's running after it. The rain's beating down.

I make my way to the side yard, catch the remaining chicken by the legs, and race with him into the cottage.

Mother's kneading dough, her head wagging. She doesn't look up at me, but she knows. Her fingers like to strangle the dough.

Keeping the chickens safe, that's a lad's job—my job. I should have repaired the chicken coop, like Mother said. I should have put them there. The rooster runs to a corner and squats; his legs disappear. At least the fox took the hen, not the rooster. Now there's no question of eggs— no cause for any more fighting.

Father's gone a long time. When he comes in, he drops four dead fox kits on the floor. "That vixen won't hunt around here anymore."

I walk over and fall to my knees beside the soft kits. I think of them playing in their den just a day ago, tumbling over one another, nipping with sharp milk teeth. I've found many dens in the springtime. I like to watch and pretend I'm a kit. Why did this vixen wait till autumn to have her kits? Did the animals get confused by the drought?

"I'll make a stew." Mother takes up the long knife. "The pelts are small, but I can use them for something. Or better, I'll sell them in town." She lifts one by the foot, slashes around the ankle, then around the other, then around both front paws. "Seems we can't do anything right. But I can do this." Her face barely moves as she talks. "We don't have fields, we don't have chickens. We've got fox kits." She slits down the belly and peels off the skin like a jacket.

I run outside, my head aching with small things that should be breathing—fox kits, Flora's brother.

The door bangs behind me. Father strides past, out to the field, right through the grazing sheep, and beyond.

Maybe it's the way he holds his head or the swing of his fists or just the length of his stride, I don't know, but I run as fast as I can, till I'm no more than fifty feet behind him, then I slow down to match his pace. Faster and faster. He doesn't know I'm here. He's heading east, toward the cliff.

The robbers live beyond that cliff somewhere. It's a lawless land. Father once said there were over a thousand of them between the two border valleys, and more joined every day of the drought—men who couldn't make a living any other way.

I stop.

He's going to join them. He's going to make us rich. "Father!" I scream. "Don't go!"

I run off the path in a shortcut and swerve at the last minute. Lord save me. I stare at the ring of mushrooms, at the matted grasses in the center. A fairy circle. A fairy's been dancing here, sure as I'm alive. If I'd rushed into the circle, I'd have been snatched into the fairy world.

Carefully I pick my way back to the path and try to
40 catch up, but now Father's climbing, crawling up the rock

face. That's crazy. If he wanted to join the robbers, he should have gone around the base of the cliff. But he's going up, up. Dark is falling and the rain won't ease off. "Stop!" I shout. "I'm sorry I left the chickens out. I'm sorry. Stop! Please! Come back."

Can't he hear me? I hear him: singing. Or raving? By the time I reach the base of the cliff, he's high above me.

How did he do that? There are so few holds, so few crevices. I move up slowly. He's so far above, he's disappeared into the fog. But I hear his song.

"Father!" I shout. "Stop!"

Is he close to the top by now? The other side of the cliff drops off into nothing.

Why climb?

He's going after the pot of gold. That's it. The end of the rainbow.

"I don't want gold," I scream. "I don't want anything. Just you."

I climb until I'm in the fog and I can't see. I'm afraid to go any farther. "Father!" I call and call and call. I hear him only faintly now.

I'm sorry for everything, everything. "Please," I'm screaming.

Lightning flashes and for several seconds I can see him, climbing steady and straight-backed. He doesn't look down. Lightning flashes again as Father stops and raises his face to the water of the skies. He sings loud and louder. And he steps out into white air.

Silence.

Not even a shout.

CHAPTER SEVEN

Seven Years Later

"Wake up, lad! Wake up!" Mother rubs my cheeks and bundles me against her. My hands run on the back of her worn shift. "Jack, my poor lost lamb." She croons and rocks.

I cling to her and smell the onions in her hair, which hangs loose around me.

"There there, lad."

Her arms and hands are hard. She works beside me all day long. We hoe Ian Hedley's fields and seed them in spring. We tend them in summer. After the grain harvest, we pick fruit at Lucky Ben's apple and pear orchards all autumn. I should be doing that work alone, and she should stay home. After all, I'm strong and fast—I do the work of three men in one day. But there's nothing for Mother to do at home; we have no grain to winnow or to brew into ale, we have no pigs to tend. And this way we both get paid, though pitiful little it is.

Still, farming is the only thing that makes me happy. It's what Father and I did together.

Father.

I grab her arm as the panic seizes me again, squeezes my chest so tight, I gasp. I have to reach him.

"Shhh." Mother pries open my fingers and stands. "Was it the same dream?"

My fingers open and close, open and close. I will them still. My heart slows. Quiets. I can breathe now. I must breathe. I cannot climb.

"Go back to sleep now." Mother hesitates. "Try to find peace, Jack. Try." She leaves.

I shut my eyes and wait for morning. But my eyelids are hot. They itch. I rub them, then open my eyes. Moonlight comes from above. I keep our roof in good repair, but I've allowed one hole in the corner over my room to stay open. In the moonlight my hands are iridescent.

I rise from the straw mat and climb out the window. My feet follow the path Father took. The ground is hard and cold at first, and small pebbles dig into my soles. Night birds cry and animals scamper in the grasses. In the distance, the white of sleeping sheep standing up in flocks catches the moonlight. I cut off the path through the heather, dodging that moon that tries to illuminate me. I am running. The plants are spongy now, a wilderness of moss.

The promontory is as steep as ever. My nails scrabble against the rock. I have to stop him before he steps into the cloud and leaves me, leaves Mother. No holds welcome my hands. Nothing helps me in this, my most important duty.

I back up a good ten yards. Then I race against the breeze of the sudden moon-dead dark, against the heat of my heart. I race and jump to climb the rock. I smash my forehead, my hands, until I crumple.

. . .

Flora sits beside me. She hums and her hands flutter about in zigzags, like swallows.

I roll in the morning dew on the grass.

"Don't be foolish, Jack. Lie flat." Flora dips a rag into a pail and puts the cool wet cloth on my forehead. I feel the brew trickle down both sides of my head, into my hair, and I smell the pennyroyal. "You made a right good mess of yourself this time."

I raise my hands in front of my eyes and slowly remember last night—how Mother cried, how the physician pressed comfrey between my fingers and wound the bandages around both my hands till they were fat and white. Now I have paws; the tips are bear claws. I growl.

"Stop that." Flora scratches beside her nose. Her black hair curls as dangerously as my claws. She tosses those curls. "I don't want to be here, you know. I have chores." She leans over me, olive eyes darker than pooled night. My mouth goes dry with longing. "This is the seventh anniversary of his death," she says. "Why can't you let it go, Jack? Mama died, little Sebastian died, just days before your father. But I've let go, Jack. I don't wallow in it like you do." She is silent for a few moments. "Why can't you be like you used to be?"

I want to comb her hair with my claws. I put my head in her lap and growl softly. I nuzzle in.

Flora pushes me off and stands. "You go most of the year like an ordinary person. Then autumn comes and you do this." She points at me. "You growl like an animal."

"We're all animals."

"Not like you, Jack. You slam yourself against the cliff."

"I try to climb it."

"Why? You can't get him back. The storm took him. Your father is gone, Jack. Nothing can bring him back."

I get on all fours and look down under me, the length of myself. I am clothed. Nothing reveals that all the parts of me are flying away, away. My wounded hands scream at me. I shift my weight and rise.

"You're sixteen, Jack. Not a child any longer." Her hands move as she talks. She stops them, clasps one within the other. "Get home. Ease your mother's burden."

I stare into her eyes. Night without clouds. "Night is the best time, Flora."

Her face softens. "You were smart once. I remember. I remember all about you." She whispers now. "You might still be the handsomest youth in the valley and maybe even the sweetest, but no one dares love a lunatic." Flora turns and walks a few steps. She looks over her shoulder. Then she goes, the bucket thumping against her leg.

Thump, wump.

She is gone.

I search back over her words. "The storm took him." That's what she thinks. That's what everyone thinks.

I walk toward home through tiny alpine flowers. Sun beats on my head.

Last night Mother found me at the foot of the cliff. I woke as she hauled me home, stumbling half on her. I stayed awake as the physician bandaged my hands and had me drink a brew made from mandrake for the pain.

Mother was kind to have the physician put me out here. She told him I love to roll in the grass—it would make me feel better. But I know she wanted me to wake to blue sky. She thought the open air would stave off the dream.

I tried to tell Father I was sorry that night so long ago. I wanted to take back my thoughtless words about the pot of gold. But I stopped halfway up the cliff. I was scared.

If I had kept on climbing, I'd have told him and everything would have been different. But I stopped, and he didn't even know I was there. I am sure of that; no father would let his son see him do what Father was about to do.

They're wrong: the storm didn't take him away.

Father gave himself. He gave himself to the clouds.

No one blamed me.

Mother says it still, every time I have the dream. Father slipped on wet stone, she says. That's all.

We couldn't find his body. Maybe it caught on a ledge

of stone. Maybe his bones lie bleached in the sunlight halfway up the promontory.

We buried his pipe and tobacco.

To this day, no one blames me. But everyone's disappointed in how I'm turning out. They'd be that much more disappointed in me if they understood that I could have stopped him if only I'd kept climbing.

I'm witness, over and over in my dreams.

What kind of fool takes his son's childish words and shapes them into a knife to pierce his own heart? I want to shake Father—I want to shake sense into him. But, then, I knew he was a fool. Mother had said it just that day. I knew it.

And I talked about gold anyway.

CHAPTER EIGHT

Cow

Mother slaps the milk bucket on the table. "Practically empty." She wipes her hands on her apron. "We'll have to ask Flora to lend us some again."

"I'll ask her." Flora's skirt swings in my mind. Her bucket swings. Morning is a good time to see Flora. Afternoon is a good time to see Flora. Night is the best time to see Flora.

"We have to sell the cow, Jack. She's only valuable as meat now."

"I'll take her to town."

Mother sinks into a chair. "You're better today. You grow crazier and crazier until September twelfth, then overnight you're sane again." She looks calm for a moment, almost serene. "All right, take her. Sell her for a good price. Don't get cheated, Jack. People always try to cheat poor folk like us. Sell her well—for a heavy purse." She looks at me with sudden decision in her eyes. "When you come back, I'll go talk to Ian Hedley. Maybe he'll buy the house from us. He can put a tenant farmer in it. He's a good man, he'll buy it, I think."

"Sell the house?" I say, stupefied.

"We'll move to town. I can take in a lot more sewing there. And you can find a job as a handyman. You're the best worker anyone's ever seen; everyone will hire you. Or you could apprentice yourself to a tanner or cobbler. We can do it. It's time for us to start a new life. Go on, Jack."

. . .

I lead the cow by a rope. Poor old girl; her udders hang loose. Whoever buys her will slice her up. Does she enjoy walking the strange market road? Has she ever minded the tedium of her life? "Moo," I say gently.

Across the field I spy Flora entering the chicken coop. I slow down. She comes out a while later, the wire basket full of eggs. It's been so long since we had our own chickens, or anything else. When Father disappeared, we had two hogs, and cows as well. But I was a boy of nine. I got paid practically nothing for my work in the Hedley fields. I gathered wild berries and nuts for selling, I sat shepherd in the rainy winter months, I helped pluck ducks and geese in the manor kitchens—but all for a pittance. By the time I got paid a man's wage, we'd already sold our livestock just to keep from starving. There's nothing left but this old cow.

I watch Flora swing the basket of eggs. She sings to herself and I catch fragments of the melody. She looks my way and waves a slender honey arm.

Flora would have married me if I hadn't changed. In a year or two we would have taken vows. We both know it when we look at each other; she can't hide it and I don't want to.

Mother's right. We need a new life. This one is as dry as the cow.

The cow clops, so I move to cow rhythm. We clop along, cow and me.

"Crazy Jack, Crazy Jack!" Lads run up to the road through the tall grass. Out of the corner of my eye I see three scrawny boys, slinking like wildcats. Stones fly, sharp on my cheek, my shoulder. "Run, crazy man." They laugh.

The cow moos.

A boy lifts an arm, stone at the ready. "You ran into the cliff last night. Don't you have the sense to run now?"

"He can't run with the cow." A second lad pulls on the arm of the first. "Let him be. Come on home. We've got stalls to muck."

The lads wander off.

Clop clop. Cow and me under the noon sun. The dust of the road billows around our ankles.

Tiny violets crowd the edge of the road, tougher than they look. If no one passed this way for a week, they'd manage to spread their way from one side to the other. Violet, violet.

Blueberry bushes curl their red-edged leaves. I know the indigo of their berries, the indigo almost as deep as the black of Flora's eyes.

A blue-tailed skink crosses a fallen log by the side of the road. My eyes trace blue streaks after him.

I hardly slept last night. I drop to the ground in the midst of wild lamb's lettuce. My fingers rest heavy on the tiny leaves as the cow chews at my side. I pull a handful and chew as well. Yellow cowslips and orange corn poppies line the road to the village.

I find the food I stashed in my pocket yesterday. A red radish. Red.

The cow nibbles beside me.

Violet, indigo, blue, green, yellow, orange, red. Colors arrange themselves before me in the rainbow. I never fail to see it. I never fail to curse it.

Time to go, Cow, I think. Time to sell you.

Cow pushes her muzzle through the cowslips. She is lost up to her eyes in the tiny flowers.

Lost farm, now lost cow.

"Isn't good for much, is she?"

The voice is songlike. I hadn't seen him walk up. He's an old man with a high-crowned hat that has so many ribbons hanging from the brim, I can't see his face. I'd be alarmed at finding a stranger here so suddenly but for the fact that I'm a strapping lad and he's bent and frail. He jerks his thumb toward the cow.

I lean forward a little. He has insulted my cow—he's

not a buyer. But he smells sweet, like he's been standing over a cauldron sugaring nuts. The August fair was last month. What brings a candyman this way now?

"Oh, I'm going to buy her, all right. I like nothing better than cream. She'll fatten up on vetch with me."

I blink.

"You heard right."

I'm dreaming, I think. I'm dreaming that this man sees my thoughts—that he talks directly to what's inside my head.

He laughs, like tinkling bells. "Well now, look at those bandages. You're the youth that slams himself against my cliff every year, aren't you?"

His cliff? That land is unclaimed. But now I'm looking at the shirt that hangs loose around him, at the britches that are held up at the waist by rope and rolled up at the bottom. The cut, the color, the size, everything; my eyes dart from one detail to the next. This is a familiar shirt, these are familiar britches. I'm trembling as I dare to look at his right shoulder. There's the stain from the seed bags. Oh, Lord.

"Found these clothes in a little heap at my doorway, practically," he says. "Years ago. Must be about seven by now."

Did you hear a ghost scream, I want to ask? Did you find bones? I go rigid with the need to grab that shirt and put it on my own back. And the britches—I want to stride boldly in those britches. They should be mine now; a boy should inherit something. I have a right to some small thing, to Father's clothes. I have a right.

"These are your father's?"

He does—he knows my thoughts—just like a sprite.

"And what else would I be? So why did you summon me, lad?"

Me summon you? But, yes, I've heard that cowslips are the link between the human world and the fairy world. And it's noon, the fairies' hour. I should have pulled Cow along. Stupid me. Most fairies appear as strong as anyone else, stout and fat-cheeked. But plenty of them resemble creatures of the elder world. His hat, his musical voice— oh, I should have known instantly.

Fairies are unpredictable. They can play wicked tricks. My skin prickles with danger.

But I haven't broken any rules: I haven't looked upon his face; I haven't spoken to him. It's not too late to escape unscathed. My fingers search the ground nearby for a four-leafed clover, something to break a fairy spell should he cast one.

"Humph. You don't even know why you called me? Well, it's your lucky day, and mine, too. I want that cow. Sell it to me and you won't need protection. Not from me, at least." He leans over and inspects Cow's ears and eyes as she continues to rip grasses. Then he laughs again. "I've been wearing these clothes too long to give them up, but I'll give you something else in return for the cow. What's your pleasure, lad?"

A heavy purse. That's what Mother told me to get. But fairies can offer much more—their generosity is legend-ary. They can offer precious stones.

"Jewels? Really?" With one bony finger he taps the bandage on my forehead. "I doubt that's your heart's deepest desire."

53

It's all I can do to stay silent. If he's a fairy, true and real, I can ask for what I need. I can ask to go back to that night, to climb the promontory without fear, to take Father's hand and lead him home.

"Ah, now that's another matter. So that's why you assault my cliff—you want to climb it, eh? Tell you what. I can't undo the past, but I can offer you this." He hands me a bag. "The full price."

My heart bangs in my chest. I pivot on my bottom so that my back is to him, and look in the bag. At beans, black like a rainy night.

Beans. Worthless. My eyes burn with disappointment. He's no fairy. I crush the bag in my hands and wave him off, being careful not to look his way, just in case.

"That bag is what you want. It was in his pocket." He takes the bag and breathes inside it. Then he dumps the contents in my lap.

Seven beans: violet, indigo, blue, green, yellow, orange, red.

They were black before. I know they were black before.

"And now they're not." The man puts his mouth close to my ear and says very softly, "Rainbow beans."

I can't listen to him, I mustn't, for Mother's sake. But my fingers play with the beans. Smooth and hard. I shake my head—I'm such a fool.

"No, you're not. You're a farmer." He whistles.

Hearing those words while knowing I'll never farm again hurts worse than the sharpest stones. But I can't let it bother me. Nothing's real. I'm sitting by the side of the 54 road with an imaginary stranger talking to my thoughts, handing me a bag of beans that his own breath colored. I should laugh at the games my head plays. Those boys were right: I'm Crazy Jack.

"Take them, Jack." He strokes the sleeve of Father's shirt. "You're a fine farmer. Plant them."

A fine farmer. That's what Father called me. That's what he taught me to be. I look down at the beans that were in Father's pocket. They shine rainbow. I hear Father saying, "Sometimes you've got to take a risk."

"Take the risk," whispers the old man.

A giddiness seizes me. My hands move on their own; they place the cow's lead in the old man's palm.

He dances off the road in a mad whirl of flutter steps, fairy steps for sure, through the grasses, the cow plodding in the green.

I run for home. The rainbow is caught in my bandaged fist. I stop and open it, trembling with fear that the beans will have vanished. Violet, indigo, blue, green, yellow, orange, red. Always that order.

I close my fist over the beans. They seem to hiss, as though they are so hot they sizzle. But my bandages protect my skin.

I'll plant this rainbow.

CHAPTER NINE

Beans

"Beans." Mother stares, turning pale. "What are you telling me?"

"I traded the cow."

"For seven beans. Beans!" She is shouting now. "No, Jack—nothing can excuse this!" She throws the beans in my face. She pounds the wall with her fists and rips at her hair. "We are lost, lost. Oh, Jack. Some evil took your senses." Her back hunches like a snail shrinking around salt. She falls to her knees.

I kneel beside her, arms encircling. "It's all right.

These beans, they're the rainbow. I'll plant the rainbow."

She pushes me away and runs from the house. Little noises crackle from her like a sputtering fire.

A finger of doubt touches my eyelids; they quiver uncontrollably. My ears buzz, shutting out the sounds of the rest of the world.

If he wasn't a fairy, if he was a real man, I can run after him, give back his beans, get back our cow. He can't be far. I can find him if I try.

Then Mother and I will move to town.

And never again work the earth.

No. I sink to my knees. That's what being lost truly means.

I hold my fingers on my eyelids to still them. Mother is too frightened to realize I did right.

A wheatear calls. I open my eyes and glance out the window to see the small bird take to the air.

I search the floor till I find all seven beans. Slowly I lay them on the windowsill, one beside the other in a straight line. They glow. I touch them gingerly, with just a fingertip. They writhe. I suck in my breath. Magic fills our home.

I scoop up the beans and find the shovel. The path takes me through the ever-warming afternoon. I keep stopping to open my hand and count the beans. Their colors burn against my white bandage.

The sheer face of the cliff rises before me, nine yards or so high. After that, one could climb easily from crag to crag. I could go where he went. But there's no way around that sheer face. How did Father do it?

Today I have no urge to throw myself at the rock. I stand as though before a shrine. I am reverent.

The fairy said this was his cliff, and I know fairies live inside hills and mountains. But the dirt at the cliff base belongs to no one, and, after all, didn't he say I should plant them?

I wiggle my toes. The dirt sends promises through my feet, up through my whole self. I dig: one hole for all seven beans, one rainbow. I dig, deep as my arm, deep as a grave. The earth is black and loamy, sweet and rich. I drop the beans, one by one: violet, indigo, blue, green, yellow, orange, red. From within the hole the beans look black. Fear snatches me. I reach in and pluck one out. Still green. I kiss the bean and it wriggles. I laugh and laugh and drop the bean, green center of the rainbow, into the light of its brothers.

I pile the dirt into the hole and smooth the top. Beans can be a good autumn crop. And now I remember: that's the crop Mother wanted to plant the day the vixen got that hen. Everything is happening as it should. I turn my face upward, eyes closed. Heavy raindrops hit here and there, coming scattered and slow at first. I open my mouth and drink.

"Jack," Flora calls. "What are you doing here again?" I sense how she comes near, though my eyes are still closed. I smell the grains in her skirt, the plum juice on her tongue. I want to taste those plums on her lips. She takes my hands and I open my eyes. "Your bandages are dirty. What were you digging for?"

"I planted the rainbow."

She sighs. "You can stand here, face to the rain, all day and all night. Why should I care? Why should anyone care if you abandon us like that?" She is silent for a moment. Her hands drop. "William wants to marry me."

No, I scream inside my head. No.

"I knew you wouldn't say anything." She blinks and looks down. "Grab your shovel and come back home, Jack. Even you can catch cold."

I pick up the shovel, obedient and stupid. If I had a rope around my neck, I'd beg her to hold the end of it. "Moo," I say to her retreating back.

"You're not a cow, Jack."

"You used to know how to play, Flora."

She turns and her eyes flash. "Your mother told me how you sold the cow. For seven beans." Flora puts her hands on her hips. "How could you?"

I slowly gather her skirts together in a ball between my hands, exposing her calves and the lower parts of her hard thighs. I give the smallest tug. She steps toward me; her eyes search mine. I smile to reassure her. "It was a good trade."

"Your mother fears a sprite duped you. It was probably Dunnie. Did he speak in verse? Don't answer—just nod."

"Shhh." I steady my voice. "Help me, Flora. Believe in the magic with me."

Her lips tremble.

I put my face close to hers.

"Beans. A handful of beans." Her face goes slack. "Oh, Jack, let me go. I can't be tied to your madness."

I open my hands.

Her skirt falls loose and she spins away.

I watch her run and know: Flora and William will be man and wife. He'll share his bed with her.

I'll share my bed with whatever dreams come.

CHAPTER TEN

The Vine

It's not yet dawn, but I rise and dress. We finished the bread at dinner and hunger sits in my stomach, so it's best I don't walk past the table. Besides, Mother could be sitting there, moaning to herself. Last night she wrapped herself in the old winnowing sheet and walked about our cottage asking, "What were you thinking of—trading the cow for beans?" Her voice was faint, as if she'd toiled a hundred years.

I climb out the window. I rip a handful of wild buckrams and stuff my cheeks. The garlic odor shoots up, makes my nostrils flare.

What's that? A hint of dawn silhouettes Flora and Mother, standing by the stone wall. Flora balances a basket on her head. She places the basket on the ground and their heads bob as they talk.

I creep and crouch behind the wagon, along its side. At just the right moment I race across the last open stretch to grab Flora about the waist. I lift her high and swing her around. I snort. I bark. I yowl.

She laughs as her hair flies in my eyes and nose and mouth. Then she stops and pushes at my locked arms. "Down, Jack. Good dog. Down."

I lower her gently, relinquish her reluctantly.

"Jack," says Mother. Her eyes cloud. She knows my love for Flora is doomed. "We've got to find work. Ian Hedley has decided to let the fields fall fallow through autumn so his geese can fatten on the stubble. And next spring he's turning his sheep out on them. He'll need fewer wage laborers that way."

I can hardly breathe as I ask, "Did you offer to sell him the house?"

She looks down. "He's not in a buying mood." Her words come slowly. "Today, Jack. We must find work today."

I nod, my face quiet, but inside I'm rejoicing that we still have our cottage; we're not leaving this earth yet.

"You're strong," she says, "and most of the year you're clever. Wash up. We're going into town together."

I stretch my neck, aware that Flora watches me. 62 Her chest rises; she cannot hide from me. If she steps closer . . . But she won't. She'll marry William. "They grew last night, Mother."

Mother narrows her eyes. "What grew?"

"The beans."

"Beans can't grow overnight. And how can it matter whether seven beans grow, anyway? Tsk."

"I planted and they grew."

"Let me see," Flora says. "Where are they, these magic plants from magic beans?"

"At the foot of the cliff."

Flora knits her brows. "Then how do you know they've grown? You just got out of bed."

"And how do you know that?"

"I saw you climb out the window." She blushes as she realizes she's been caught watching for me. Her eyes dart away for a moment. "How can you possibly know what's happened to the beans?"

I smile. "I felt the roots and sprouts."

"You felt them?"

"In my eyeballs."

Flora looks at Mother and shakes her head.

Mother has her fists on her temples. "All right, Jack. You're still not well. I can't take you to town talking like that. Who'd hire you? I'll go alone. You go to Flora's father and beg him to let you help with the chores in exchange for milk and cheese. That's all. Milk and cheese. He can't say no if that's all you ask for. He's not a rich man, but he can afford enough milk and cheese to keep us alive." She turns and walks toward the road.

"Come with me, Flora."

Flora steps backward, away from me. "Where?"

"I'll show you the bean plants."

"Is that what you were doing yesterday, when you said you planted the rainbow?" She hugs herself with both arms, takes another step backward. "William is coming by."

"William eats flies."

Flora pushes me in the chest. Her cheeks flame. "He does not."

"He's a toad."

She opens her mouth. Then snaps it shut. Her eyes burn. "He's sensible. And he wants me, Jack. He doesn't care about my Spanish skin."

"I love your Spanish skin."

She flushes. "Don't be difficult. You know what I mean."

"You want to spend the rest of your life grateful to a sensible toad?"

Flora pushes me with both hands now. "You're an outsider yourself these days, Jack. Why can't you understand?" Her eyes glisten. She pushes again.

I grab both her wrists. "Come and see with me." I'm praying that there's truly something to see—something, anything—but I don't let my prayer enter my voice. "This time you be the witness."

"Witness?"

"To a miracle." I pull her along.

"I'll come. Just let go of my hands." She looks over her shoulder, every which way. "If someone tells William, he might not think well of me."

"There's no one to see. Everyone else is still in bed."

But I let go. A woman's reputation can be swept away like

a spiderweb. Small lads might call names and throw stones at her. Still, I'm reeling from the touch of her skin. I point to the rise near her house. "Remember when we kissed behind your woodpile?"

"We were children, Jack."

I see the smock she wore. "Remember when you showed me—"

"Jack! Stop it. You're the one who spoiled everything." She shakes her head. "Just hurry. William needs to find me at work in the dairy." Flora runs a few paces. "Hurry up, will you?"

I stride long, my eyes on the path ahead.

And now I see darkness. The gray rock has turned black. But as we come closer I see that it's not black, after all, but a deep forest green.

We're running.

The dark stalk climbs, thick around as a pine sapling. Its tendrils curl into crevices, like fingers. The massive leaves are flat and shiny and heart shaped. I pant and look up and up and up; the beanstalk stretches beyond the clouds. I squint against the rising sun that glints from those leaves in violet, indigo, blue, green, yellow, orange, red. The light breaks, showering us both.

Flora puts her hand out toward the stalk, but she doesn't touch it. "Oh, Jack. Over there." She points to clusters of bean pods. "So many. And huge. Oh!" She throws her arms around me, breathless. I press her to me. But she pulls away, worry squinching her face. "What if someone else planted it?"

"I planted it, Flora. Who else would plant here? It grew from the beans."

"A beanstalk can't grow this size overnight."

"You were here yesterday. You saw no beanstalk then. Your own eyes tell you, Flora."

Flora looks dazed. Then she laughs. "What am I saying? No ordinary beanstalk can grow this size ever." She breathes heavily and looks up the stalk. "You were right, Jack," she says slowly. "You were right to trade the cow for beans. I don't know how you knew, but you did. This stalk alone can feed you and your mother for a long time."

I finger a leaf and put one hand around the side of the stalk. Then the other. The draw of the vine overpowers me. "It's not the pods that matter, Flora."

"What?" Flora comes so close her heat caresses my cheek. "Jack?"

I climb where Father went, only I have the beanstalk as my ladder, the leaf stems strong as rungs. A fairy ladder. But the bandages on my hands make me clumsy. I hold on with my left hand and sink my teeth into the cloth that covers my right. With a jerk of my head, the bandage rips and falls to the ground. I do the same to the left.

"Wait," calls Flora. "I'll be back with the basket. Don't go higher than you have to."

I climb.

"Wait, for Heaven's sake," she shouts. "I'll be back. I'll help you gather them. You can sell them in town."

I climb without looking down.

CHAPTER ELEVEN

Another
Hen

I passed the sheer rock face long ago. If I wanted, I could be sprinting up the cliff now. I could go from that crag to that crag to that crag over there. But I prefer the beanstalk.

I break off a leaf, hold my arm out away from the rock, and let it fall, zig and zag, down out of sight. This is the seventh leaf I've dropped. Will Flora gather the heart-shaped leaves?

I cannot see her, because I am surrounded by fog. I

wouldn't even be sure the stalk was here if my hands didn't hold it tight.

I climb. It feels like hours, but the sun eludes me, so I cannot be sure. The stalk finally thins and I'm near the top at last. If I continue, the stalk could break; I could fall into cloud. Easy.

I put one foot out for the rock. No rock. No rock. It was here before—I saw it—it was here. The vine clung to the cliff—the crags were within my reach. But my foot can't find it now. I thrust a hand into the wet white. Nothing. The vine goes heavenward on its own.

I think of the elfin bean man—of how he whispered my own thoughts, whispered, "Take the risk." My blood stops.

I step out.

Spongy air holds me, like peat on the moors. I paddle slowly through white and my heart dares to beat again. Nothing but white, dizzying white. I close my eyes and squash my fists into my stomach to steady it. My hands throb.

"Who goes there?"

I turn abruptly to the voice, opening my eyes. "Jack," I say to the white wall.

"Jack?" The voice is female, eager. "Come closer, Jack."

"Where? I can't see you."

"Turn right, Jack. Keep coming."

The ground firms under my feet. I press a little, then more, to make sure. The fog clears gradually. I hear bleating, and puffs of cloud solidify into fleece. The enor-
68 mous flock extends as far as I can see, grazing in clumps

of two or three on dark heather. The lanolin of their wool oils the heavens.

I am on a slate path. Normal, everyday slate. I go weak. Only slate. Only sheep. But ahead is an immense door, half again as high as our cottage door; in the doorway is a tall woman. I approach, each step slower than the last.

"How did you get here?" It is exactly what I want to ask her, but her fierce eyes silence me. She holds the door frame with both hands as though she's keeping herself from charging.

I stop, out of her reach. "Are you real?"

"Are you?"

I slap my palm on my chest so she can hear the thump. My wounded hand! I flinch.

The woman tilts her head back and looks down on me. "You're not big enough to jump the divide."

"What divide?"

"The one between this cliff and the north one."

The great escarpment, she means. "That divide is too wide for anyone to jump," I say.

"So how did you get here?"

"I climbed."

She gasps. "But no one can climb to the top. Ever since . . ." Her eyes change; a veil descends. Her face grows cool. "How old are you, little liar?"

"I'm not a liar."

"Then tell me how you really got here."

Why does it matter? Who is this woman? I put my hands in my pockets and wait.

The woman smiles and drops her arms. Her lips are darkened, like those of the women of town. She leans 69 against the door frame, one hip jutting out, her light hair wispy and glowing. She is a willow, clothed in the finest white dress I've ever seen.

I look up at the looming house, more castle than house. How is it I've never heard of this place?

"Cat got your tongue?" She laughs. "Come in, Jack. You're starving."

How does she guess my hunger?

The smell of bacon wafts from within and I lunge past her, down the long corridor lined with barrels of salted meats all the way into a large hall. A feast is set out on a high table. Muffins in a haze of sweet spice. Roasted potatoes and onions. In the center a platter piled high with that aromatic bacon, and sausages and chops and ham. So much food makes me shy, as though I'm seeing something obscene.

The woman stands close beside me. My head is level with her shoulder. She touches the bandage on my forehead exactly where the fairy touched it. "How did you get hurt?"

"My head slammed into a rock."

"A ruffian, are you? Well, I know how to deal with ruffians." She brushes the hair back from my cheek. "Satisfy yourself, Jack. Now."

I shrink from her icy fingers. I've heard about women like this—town women who know things a girl like Flora doesn't know. My eyes turn back to the sausages on the table and I sit on the edge of the only chair. It is enormous—way too tall for the woman. My feet swing above the ground.

She loads my plate with fragrant meats and slides the

basket of muffins toward me. "Take, Jack. As many as you like."

This has to be magic, but the food looks like food should look. Especially the meat. It's been so long since I've eaten hearty. And I begin. Lovely sausages. Sweet muffins. Hot potatoes swimming in salty juice from the meat.

I gulp honey wine.

She smiles and sits on the table beside my plate, her knees by my elbow. She crosses slim legs and wiggles long toes. Her fragility takes me by surprise—thin skirt falling over thin hips, narrow waist. She smells like roses in full bloom.

I chew dutifully, but the hunger has been appeased already. My eyes climb to her breasts, hidden under the flowing cloth, but close, so close.

She cocks her head at me. "There's one thing you should know." She hesitates.

My heart clutches and I jump from the huge chair.

She puts both hands on my shoulders and presses down. "He's not here yet. But when he comes, you must hide."

"Who?" I ask, though I know he's the man whose meat I've been eating, whose woman she is. He is the man who fits in this chair.

"You'll find out soon enough. For now, eat your fill, Jack. Then you must hide yourself outside, hide your smell among the sheep. He's been out all night scavenging, so he'll be ferociously hungry. I'll feed him. He'll drink himself into a stupor and sleep the rest of the morning. Then you and I can talk." She smiles. "Get to know   71 one another. You can help me." She wipes juices from my chin and licks her finger clean. "Trust me."

I back away as I press my sleeve to my mouth. "I trust no one who lives in a castle above the clouds."

A great thud shakes the floor.

"Fee!" a voice thunders from outside. "Fi!" The voice booms close. "Fo!" The front door bangs open. "Fum!" The stone walls ring. "I smell the blood of an Englishman." Steps pound down the corridor, closer, closer.

The woman slips off the table and runs across the room to a shelf. With amazing strength she turns over a huge pottery bowl. "Climb under! Quick!"

I leap onto the shelf. She lifts the edge of the bowl and I crawl under and squat. The bowl smells heady, of bread yeast. Sweat beads over my entire body.

"Be he live or be he dead, I'll grind his bones to make my bread. Where is he? Where is the Englishman?"

"If you want to eat an Englishman again, you'll have to carry him here on your shoulder," she says.

I clench my teeth to keep them from rattling. Cannibals. Did she bathe in rosewater to cover the scent of human blood? Has she hidden me now only to eat me later when she's alone?

Feet stomp around the room. "That other one came on his own."

"No one can climb the cliff now that you shaved the top ten yards smooth all the way around. It's impossible."

Loud sniffs.

"The smell is fresh and strong. There's a man in this room."

My fingers dig into my cheeks in terror.

"It's the pork," comes the woman's silky tone. "Bacon and sausage. Sit down and eat, my love."

"Who's been at this meat, at these muffins?"

She laughs a small laugh. "I couldn't wait. Are you angry?"

"It's good." He chews loudly. "Good."

"Good mead," she says with a giggle.

Loud slurps.

"I brought home an ox."

"I'll tie it up before it wanders away in the fog and falls off the cliff." The woman's voice is slightly slurred.

"Stay here. It's dead."

More slurps.

Sweat pours down my face. Here all flesh is as one—the pig, the ox, me. Nausea rises in my throat.

"And I brought something else, too."

"What is it?" Her voice goes high with excitement. "Oh, oh, it's lovely. And it suits my hand perfectly."

"Bring my hen," says the cannibal.

I hear the woman rush from the room, then back.

Muted clucks.

"Lay, you bag of feathers. Lay." He orders it twelve times. "Bring the basket."

I hear the woman running again.

More eating noises. Slower.

And then I hear small thunder. Evenly spaced; somehow familiar. Finally I understand: this is snoring. With great effort I lift the edge of the bowl and peek. An enormous man sits at the table, his head collapsed onto his folded arms.

The giant!

The woman is nowhere to be seen.

The giant's back is as wide as three men's. His head is heavier than any ox's. His massive arms would crush me.

A hen clucks and walks around the floor aimlessly, pecking here and there, clucking. And—gold! Gold gleams on the table.

I work my way out from under the bowl and drop silently to the floor. The door is across the room, beyond the table. I step softly.

Gold eggs lie on the table. I stare: twelve. The same number as the times the giant commanded, "Lay."

In an instant I grab the hen by both legs, hold her upside down so she won't squawk, and run from the house, leaping over the dead ox outside the door.

I lose myself in the fog.

CHAPTER TWELVE

Eggs and Beans

I climb down so fast I am near to falling, crashing from stem to stem.

Flora stands at the bottom, cradling beans in her apron. "Jack," she cries. "Where . . ."

I grab her hand and run. The chicken swings at my other side as I listen for the giant. I shudder so hard that I can barely stay on the path.

"How on earth did you find a chicken on the cliff?" Flora's breath is short now, too. "Ahhh," she cries.

"Whose chicken is that, Jack? Did you meet someone up there?" She yanks her hand away.

I spin and face her.

"Did you steal it?"

"From the giant," I say.

Flora shakes her head in disbelief. "The giant? The giant lives up there?"

"In a towering castle. He comes up the slope of the north cliff, then jumps the divide to the top of our promontory."

"You saw him?"

I nod.

"And you stole his chicken? Oh, Jack, how could you incur the wrath of the giant? Run now, run!"

"No." My heart grows as quiet as the heather; a sense of rightness blankets me. "If it were an ordinary chicken, I'd have never taken it, Flora. But it's part of the magic. I was meant to take it. See? The giant isn't following. It's all right, Flora. We'd hear him, I swear."

Flora blinks. "I don't understand, Jack." She looks back toward the cliff. Then she walks on in silence.

I look down at the hen. Her beak is tannish orange, but it wasn't that color before. I glance at Flora. She is all her usual colors, right down to those pink-red lips.

I turn the hen right side up and tuck her under my arm. She perches there, stupid. Chickens aren't usually docile. Perhaps she is particularly brainless. Or perhaps being swung upside down has scrambled what brains she has.

We are finally outside my cottage. Flora stops and looks at me sideways. "You were gone a long time, Jack. I
76 worried."

William might have come and gone by now. But still she stayed at the base of the beanstalk and worried about me. "Thank you." I move to kiss her cheek.

She pushes my lips away with one finger, her other hand clutching the corners of the apron together. "I'll help you pick pods tomorrow morning, if you want to go early. There are so many beans, you need extra hands. But you have to promise not to disappear again like that."

I'm ready to promise Flora anything, but I remember words overheard in that castle in the sky and already a question sprouts in the back of my mind. I must be ready to visit there again. I hold my tongue.

We enter the cottage. Flora unloads the contents of her apron onto the table.

"No, it can't be." I put my hands in the pile of beans. "They are the size of regular bean pods."

She steps back. "They looked huge on the stalk, didn't they? That beanstalk plays tricks with the eyes. As soon as I picked the pods, I could see that." Flora walks to the table, transfixed. "Maybe your eyes were tricked into thinking you saw the giant, when all you saw was an ordinary man."

Her face is so hopeful, I stay silent.

"Well, it doesn't matter that these beans are just normal size. There are so many of them. You've got plenty to sell." She's at the door.

"Stay for an egg, at least."

"A hen won't lay with anyone watching."

I smile. I cannot wait to see Flora's face as I hand her the first gold egg. I place the hen on the table. "Lay," I order.

77

The hen clucks and pecks at a bean pod. But she squats and an egg rolls from her bottom. I stare. An ordinary brown egg.

Flora takes my arm. "What a strange bird. No nest, no place to roost. Yet she laid that egg."

"I told her to."

"Don't be silly, Jack. Hens won't follow orders."

"She did." I am thinking back to the giant's words. Did he say anything special, anything to make her lay a gold egg?

"Then do it again, Jack."

At last I remember: The giant insulted the bird. "Lay, you bag of feathers," I say. "Lay, lay, lay."

One, two, three, four more eggs roll from the hen's bottom and still she pecks, oblivious.

Brown eggs.

Flora laughs. "You'll be eating eggs for the rest of your life." She laughs louder. "Or, rather, for the rest of this hen's life."

I set the eggs in a basket, then scoop the chicken up. I hold her toward the light that streams through the window. "Hen, you laid gold eggs before. But here you give only brown eggs. What is it?" I set her on the floor.

The hen clucks and pecks at nothing.

"Gold eggs?" says Flora.

"They were gold, Flora. When the hen laid eggs for the giant, they were gold. I swear." Perhaps the eggs are special inside those ordinary shells. I grab a bowl and crack the eggs. Yellow yolks. Clear whites. "I've been cheated."

Flora touches my arm. "Jack?"

I shake my head at the eggs in the bowl. "You don't understand. They were real gold."

"Jack, look at me."

I turn to Flora.

"These eggs are good. You're blessed, Jack." She talks slowly, with deliberation. "This is much better than if the hen laid gold eggs."

"Don't humor me, Flora."

"I'm not. What could you do with gold eggs but sell them? If you had to haggle over gold eggs every day, your mother would worry endlessly about being cheated. And if people knew you had a hen that laid gold eggs, she'd soon be stolen."

"Just as I stole her from the giant."

Flora nods.

"You're right."

She smiles, then ducks out the door.

I pick the hen up again and smooth her feathers.

Mother comes in a moment later. "Where did that hen come from?" She spies the bowl of cracked eggs. "She laid eggs and you cracked them." Mother looks around the floor. "All of them? You left not a single one for tomorrow?" She shakes her head. Her eyes go beyond me to the mound of bean pods on the table. She walks to them slowly.

I sit in the chair, still stroking the hen. "Eggs and beans for as long as we want."

Mother drops onto the other chair. "How, Jack?"

"The beans that I got in exchange for the cow. They grew into a colossal stalk."

She lifts beans and lets them fall through her hands.

Then she leans back in the chair, shaking her head. "Beans don't yield overnight."

"These did, Mother."

She speaks in a whisper. "Hens don't grow from beans."

"She belonged—"

"I don't want to know!" Mother sighs. "Jack, I'm tired. Don't give me more bad news."

"She'll lay however many we need."

Mother points at each yolk in the bowl. "Five eggs in one day. She's quite a layer, she is." She slits the seam of a beanpod with her nail and runs her thumb down the inside. She pops a bean into her mouth. "All these pods in one day."

"And there will be just as many tomorrow. And the day after. And as long as we want." My faith is strong. Flora was right. She's been right about everything—about rain and a rainbow and the beans and the hen. Tomorrow morning we can go picking again, and Flora can sing. "We can trade beans for cheese and milk, Mother. We can trade eggs for flour and oil."

Mother looks at me strangely. "Such hope." She rubs her thighs through her shift. "I couldn't find work, though. I tramped all over. My feet hurt. My legs hurt."

"You'll be busy here, Mother. We'll sell enough beans to buy back the fields. We'll have land to work."

She sighs. "I pray you're right."

CHAPTER THIRTEEN

The Field

A month goes by.

I stand in the field and nudge a plant with my big toe. Two hundred rows of bean plants running the width of the field, set apart just enough so that we can walk between them. Each curls a leaf the size of a thumbtip toad to the midday sun. These are ordinary bean plants, growing at the ordinary rate. I turn my face to the sun, eyes closed, and laugh in gratitude.

Every morning Mother and I go to the rock and pick bushels of beans. We take the long way around, because

Mother fears others will discover the beanstalk, even though no one goes near the land beneath the cliff. The bean pods still appear huge on the stalk, then rest small in our hands.

We set aside some for drying, to store in the earthenware jars that have stood empty so long. But I load most of them into huge bags and hang them across the back of the horse we just bought. Mother leads the mare to market, where she sells and trades all afternoon. I wave her off and go out to work the field. Our land.

We arranged with Hedley to buy back one field, just one, this season. He let us use the land on good faith, for we had no money, but he demanded half our harvest in addition to the payments.

At first we borrowed one of Flora's father's horses. But by the end of the second week, we had earned enough to buy our own horse. The third week we gave Hedley the first payment. And yesterday we paid the second quarter. Hedley was astonished. We'll pay in full long before the harvest. Next spring we can buy back the other field.

I love farming. I repaired the old plow and prepared this earth. Then I planted the beans, one to each hole, as careful as an ant, harrowing the mounds with my hands. I cut sticks and tied them into tall cones over each mound, so that the bean vines can twine up them, greedy for the sun. When I farm, I feel Father's spirit near. These plants honor his memory.

Mother and Flora come often and walk the rows. They never know what to expect. But I know. I knew these plants would be ordinary, just as the hen lays brown eggs.

Right away Mother decided that we shouldn't count on

the abundance of the beanstalk. She said, "The Lord helps those who help themselves. This field is how we help ourselves." I know she worries about the source of all this magic. But she never speaks of it. Instead, every evening she says, "You've done a good job, Jack." And she touches my shoulder less hesitantly each day.

At first Mother talked of buying a side of beef, a shank of mutton—to make what Father used to call "proper meals." I told her it was better not to, that we should show reverence to the beanstalk and the hen. I didn't tell her that the thought of meat, of spilling an animal's blood, puts me back under the bread bowl, trembling as I hear again the giant and his woman talking about an Englishman who climbed the cliff. An Englishman he ate. I've told Mother nothing at all of the giant.

So we eat eggs and beans, cheese and fruits. We chew dark bread and tell stories in the dusk. And most nights when I wake from my nightmare of teeth coming at the soft belly of a man, I manage not to scream.

One nightmare replaced the other. I don't know which is worse.

But it's daytime now—nightmares are held at bay. I'm standing in the sunlight on the good dirt that has absorbed so much of my sweat.

I whistle as I look around at the field. I will finish this job today. Then the sun and the rain and time will do their part. Nature is good.

Magic is better.

Flora is best.

I look down and there's a bright red feather at my feet. I don't know if it's a scarlet tanager's or a summer tanager's, but Flora will know, and this is just the excuse I've been looking for. I snatch it and run up the row and along the path. I leap the crumbling stone wall, duck under the laundry hanging white and bright beside Flora's home.

"Hey!" William jumps to his feet.

I stop and look past him. No Flora. It's just me and this big toad. Flora has not yet agreed to marry him, but persistence usually wins, I know that much. And William is renowned for his persistence.

I plant my feet and rock back on my heels. "You did a fine wash, William."

William's face freezes. "Flora did the wash."

What a dolt. He doesn't know I tease him. And Flora is about to pass her life with this humorless lump. "Eaten any good flies lately?"

William scratches his chin. He's caught on at last. "I'd take offense if you weren't a half-wit. What are you doing here?"

"Inspecting laundry." I put my face into a wet sheet and breathe in the suggestion of Flora's skin.

William laughs. I cannot tell if he is good-natured or nervous. I don't want him to be good-natured. I want to dislike him. I've seen him here four times this month, walking with her, leaning toward her. He is taller than me, almost as tall as the giant's woman.

Flora seems intent on whatever William says. No matter how many bushels of beans the beanstalk yields, Flora won't give me a glance; she won't tell William to go away.

I asked her once, "What can William offer?"

84   She said, "Everything."

Yet she comes to walk the field I've sown. Every day.

"What is everything?" I ask now.

William looks confused. He shuffles his feet. "I'm building a home with a large hearth."

I jerk to attention. I have wanted to build Flora a home since I was a child. Now this man is doing it. Pride shines in his eyes. This house is his gift to Flora. Flora the workhorse. Flora the cook. A house with a large hearth. "And will you have wide shelves and a huge bread bowl?" Big enough for me to hide under?

William shrugs. "Our home will have everything."

Everything. Of course.

"You're looking healthy, Jack." His voice is cautious. "Still thin as a beanstalk, but healthy."

Yes, I am lean and strong like my beanstalk. I stretch both arms upward. No heart-shaped leaves sprout from my fingertips. Yet my heart would fill my body and burst out everywhere if it could.

"Flora's father says you've been planting beans."

I drop my arms, but I stay silent. I can tell he hasn't finished.

"He says you're a good worker." William sniffs. "If you stay healthy and if you work hard, maybe I can use your help."

My help? "What kind of help does a toad need?"

William frowns. "You can't call your future employer a toad, even if you are addle-brained. I'd like to practice charity with you, Jack. Flora seems to hold sincere fondness for you. So I'd be glad to help you and your mother out a bit. But you've got to show respect."

It is not William's words so much as his tone: he talks 85

as if he is master and I am beast. But even a beast is worthy. I smile and moo loudly.

William jumps back.

I laugh and neigh.

Flora rounds the corner of the house. "Oh, Jack." I see a moment of struggle in her eyes. Please, Flora, I am begging in my head, please ask what I was doing. Please ask why. But she smiles and says, "I'm ready. Let's go, William." She comes forward briskly.

William takes her by her elbow. He accompanies her to his horse-drawn cart, looking over his shoulder at me. I smile at him, a big open smile sure to make his nerves jangle. Flora perches on the bench seat. William climbs up beside her, takes the reins.

Flora twists around and calls, "If you need something, Jack, Papa will be back soon."

I see a satisfied William easing into bed with her, belching, loud in his contentment. Are her eyes open? Or does she shut them and pretend it's me, my hands knowing her, my heart seeking hers? "There's more to life, Flora," I call.

The horse is moving, trotting.

I am running beside the cart.

Flora leans toward me. "What did you say?"

I hold up the red feather. "There's more to life," I call, "more to life than having everything."

Flora takes the feather and knits her brows in the way I love. "Go home, Jack."

The horse canters.

My breath comes in bursts as I run even with the cart.
86 "Much more."

William frowns and snaps the whip over the horse's withers until it gallops.

"Rainbows," I shout. "Rainbows." I stand in a cloud of dust. Their backs are straight, side by side.

I turn on my heel and race back to Flora's house. I pull a shutter half open, so that it's perpendicular to the wall, and use it to spring to the roof. I climb lightly to the center and stand with my feet straddling the peak. I shout, "Rainbows!"

Flora looks back.

"Rainbows!"

They are gone.

I realize both arms are above my head. I tuck them in my armpits. William must be telling her I'm a lunatic. That's what she fears. That's why she turns from me.

And maybe I am. As long as I have these nightmares, maybe I can't be anyone but Crazy Jack.

I jump from the roof, land on all fours, roll. I run and run, all the way to the beanstalk. I climb from crook to crook. It's so easy, I could climb forever. And I could fall forever, too.

But I need the answer to that one question, that one haunting question. "Take the risk," I whisper to myself. Take the risk.

CHAPTER FOURTEEN

Gold

The sun beats on my head, and sweat makes the waist-band of my trousers slip and slide as I climb. So strangely hot for October. But I'm getting closer to the sun as I climb, after all. And it is just past noon, the hottest time of day.

Yet the cloud cover stays thick under me. Indeed, it seems to grow, so that it is always just under my feet.

I imagine her voice. I remember her hip outlined in her skirt, the way her hair swings to cover one eye. I climb more quickly and the heat intensifies. My cheeks are aflame now and my breath comes in pants. I cannot close my mouth or I'll gasp. Sweat steals my grip. I look down. All I see is the clouds that rise as my feet rise.

I rub one hand on my shirt, but the shirt hangs limp with sweat. My foot slicks off the leaf stem and flies into open space.

I throw myself around the beanstalk as I fall. My arms and legs hook over the leaf stems.

I climb again, slowly, carefully. The beanstalk thins. I hold tighter. I can make it.

There is no landmark to tell me when I have reached the right height. But a moment more and my fingers will blister. No choice, no choice but one.

Breathless, I let go and surrender myself to the cloud.

The cloud disappears in an instant and I walk on sandy ground. It scorches my soles and lets off steam. I run, gasping as I lift my feet to escape the burning ground.

"Jack!"

I can't see her for the sweat in my eyes, for the hovering blackness; I am about to faint.

Her fingers close around my wrist. "This way, Jack. Come."

We run together, the pain in my feet hobbling me. As if in answer to a prayer, a gentle drizzle begins, a drizzle that would make me feel I'm in familiar territory if I let myself be fooled.

The ground becomes moss now, cool, wet, sweet beneath my singed feet. I fall and roll.

"Look, Jack."

A rainbow shines through the drizzle. It fills the sky and dances like a dervish.

She laughs. Her dress slips off one shoulder, exposing fair, smooth flesh. Her eyes are brazen. She sits up and looks down at me. "You were running so fast, you almost passed it."

I sit as well. "I love rainbows."

"Rainbows? What are you talking about?"

Can't she see it? "What, then? What did I almost pass?"

She giggles and crosses one leg over the other; her skirt swings. I see a glimpse of thigh, but, oh, a dark bruise. She flicks the skirt to cover herself and now I notice the enormous jewel on her finger. It was not there last time. "Look." She points beside me.

I get up and stand astounded before the black pot. It brims with gold nuggets the size of fists. The pot at the end of the rainbow.

"Isn't that what you came for? His gold?"

"This isn't his." I shake my head. "How could this be his?"

"Who else's would it be?" She wags a finger. "You've come to steal his gold. Admit it."

"I'm not a thief."

She puts her hand over her mouth, then sighs. "He forbade me to leave the house after the hen disappeared. He said he wanted to protect me. Both of you are terrible liars." She looks down at her hands. "You would have come and taken the gold and left, and I would have missed you entirely if I hadn't been out walking and heard your gasp. I would have missed a second chance."

"A second chance at what?" Her clothing reveals all; she can't be carrying a knife. Still, I stand ready to fight.

She reaches for the pot handle.

I push her hand away.

"It's easier together. We can hide it behind the bush by the front door."

I'll take it home, I will. I lift the pot and stagger; I can't bear such weight on my burned feet. I put it down and step from foot to foot.

"Did you think you could manage on those sore feet? And with an empty stomach, on top of it?"

"I ate breakfast." I place one hand on my full stomach. But for some reason it feels empty.

She smiles. "Breakfast was hours ago. If you're going to carry that pot, you need to eat."

"I don't eat meat anymore." Can you understand that, cannibal monster?

She cocks an eyebrow. "So you've changed your ways, my handsome thief. That's all right. I know what you need. And I'll minister to your burned feet, too."

I close both hands on the pot handle; I will not be taken in by her wiles.

She laughs. "I've got fresh bread at home. New lettuce and juicy beets. Berries from the woods. With clotted cream. A king's midday meal. How does that sound now, my sweet man? My king."

I should recoil. But she is running a finger across my lips and I am dazed, instantly famished. Against all reason, I extend the handle of the pot; we carry it together along the grassy ground to the castle steps. We set the pot behind the bush.

"Where is he?" I ask as she leads me into the hall. The cold stone of the floor is so good on my burns, so wonderful.

"On the other side of the divide, as always. It's easy to rob homes in the morning—while farmers are out in the fields. We'll hear him when he comes home. Like last time. But he's not due back yet."

I imagine him jumping the divide. It has to be fifteen feet across. How easily he could crush me.

But we are at the table—and it's set already.

"Grains, fruits, vegetables, Jack. See?" Her arm brushes my shoulder. She takes away a platter and hides it under the table. "Your chair, sire. Eat first. Then I'll fetch salve for your feet."

The beets lie in their pungent juices. I climb onto the giant's chair, let my poor feet swing free, and reach for a berry.

She slaps my hand away. "My turn, Jack." She holds a berry just inches from my lips. "Eat."

The wet berry glistens. I lean toward her hand and eat. "More."

She feeds me, berry by berry. Then she fills my goblet with apple ale and holds it to my lips.

I drink.

She takes the platter out from under the table. It holds roast beef. "Have a bite." With the long shiny blade she slices.

I cannot understand how I didn't smell the meat before.

"This is what men need. This is what you toil for. But you won't have to toil anymore. You'll be rich with his gold. You can have anything you want."

The words feel like a distant song, meaningless, as though I'm drunk. But the smell of the meat comes through. It takes all my strength to resist.

She giggles. "You're happy with this food. So now, Jack, now you'll help me. This time you'll help me, won't you?"

I stiffen. I want to ask how, but I have another question pressing on me, the question that made me return here. "Tell me something. Another man climbed here once."

"Yes," she says hesitantly. "Years ago. He filled his pockets with the giant's beans."

"Describe him to me."

Her eyes flicker. She lowers her chin and looks up at me coyly. "First, promise to help me. Take me away with you. That's what he was going to do, poor soul."

Thud! The ground shakes. "Fee!" bellows the voice from my nightmares. "Fi! Fo!" And the door bangs open. "Fum!"

We look at each other in panic.

He stamps down the corridor, faster, faster. "I smell the blood of an Englishman."

"Hide!" She runs to a wooden barrel and lifts the lid.

The voice booms behind me: "Be he live or be he dead, I'll grind his bones to make my bread."

CHAPTER FIFTEEN

Stones

"Where is he?" Furniture clatters and bangs. "Where?"

"Your hunger rules your head." Her voice is desperate.

All I can think of is his huge jagged teeth, his gaping mouth. I curl my arms tighter around my legs. Let this barrel not be a coffin.

She speaks loudly. "The beets are savory. Taste them."

"Get that out of my face!" Stomps. Sniffs. "The air is succulent," he says. "I smelled that once before—when my hen disappeared. The bread bowl teased me for weeks." Pottery breaks.

I imagine the bowl shattered on the floor. I imagine my own head shattered on the floor.

"Shame on you." I hear wood scrape. "Sit in your chair. I'll feed you well." She gives a screechy laugh. "Let's fill your belly, tame that hunger. See these lovely berries?"

"Human food." Disgust slimes his ghastly voice. "You think I am nothing more than an overgrown human? You silly human woman."

"You are much better than any human could be. Eat, eat this glorious meal. Food fit for only you." Her voice grows affectionate. "Have a seat, won't you?"

"That smell is here. That meat smell."

"The roast, it's the roast."

Sharp panic shoots through my legs and arms, up my back, my neck. I realize now that his cry is always about smell. I press my lips to my kneecap to hold in my breath.

Lumbering steps come toward the barrel. I can smell him, too, right through the wood. I can smell his murderous, hairy hand as it reaches for the handle of the lid.

Wood creaks and the giant groans. Oh, merciful sounds: he has lowered himself into the tall chair. I lift my head from my knee. Sweat soaks my britches, rolls down into the oats.

"What happened to my hen, then?"

"That hen was always wandering off. She probably came to the edge of the cliff and thought she could fly. Dumb bird. Here, try these—fresh berries."

Crash!

She whimpers.

"I want flesh."

"The beef is bloody," she wheedles, "just as you like it."

"Fresh flesh."

"Fresh flesh?" Now she flirts. "That you can have any time."

"That's right. First one, then the other." Crockery scrapes on the table. "Who's been at this meat?"

"I couldn't help it." She giggles loudly. "You know how I am. I couldn't wait."

Slurps. "Good." He smacks his lips as he eats. Interminable smacking and grunting. Finally I hear his chair rasp the floor as he pushes back from the table. "Have a look at this."

"Ah! It's beautiful. How it shines!"

"Put it on." He belches.

I hear a faint tinkling, jangling. "This is the best gift yet."

"Now, my fresh meat."

I put my hands over my ears. Still, I think I can hear moans. Moans and cries. I press my hands harder until the palms form a suction and all I can hear is the swoosh of my own blood. When they finish, will he lift his gargantuan head and smell me still? Fear shakes me until the barrel tips and gyrates on its base. Oh, Lord. I scrape my raw feet against the grains below so that pain will divert me from terror and I can stop this terrible shaking.

But with pain comes the memory of the bruise on her thigh. I should burst from this barrel and grab her away.

We could make a run for it. But I am squeezed in and the best I could do is wriggle out. He'd hear me before I got free of the barrel.

Still, that bruise. I must try.

I lower my hands and hear the thunder of his snore. It's over.

I lift the lid.

They are sprawled on the massive table, his cheek completely covering her belly, one arm raised above his head and across her chest. His drool puddles on her skin and his eyeballs look like fists under those twitching eyelids. I know his ugliness in sleep is only a hint of it awake. How on earth will I get her away without waking him?

She turns her head to me. Her eyes shine as bright as the jewels around her neck. Her fingers move to the necklace. Then she holds her hand up, the back of it facing me, fingers spread. The necklace matches the ring. She covers her face with that hand and with her other she strokes the giant's cheek.

He grunts. In his sleep his huge hands tighten into sledgelike fists.

I can save no one but myself, and even that is only with luck.

I creep past the sack on the floor, the one I am sure holds his plunder. The door swings open on silent hinges and I slide through. She called me a thief and, yes, I will take that pot of gold. But it isn't the giant's gold. He stole it. So it might as well be the gold at the end of the rainbow. I kneel by the bush.

No pot.

My heart lurches. I scramble around under the bush.

No pot, no pot. I risked everything for naught! And, oh, there it is. Foolish me. The glitter tantalizes.

I pull it to me. It is heavy indeed, but I won't leave empty-handed; I won't panic and race for the beanstalk.

I grit my teeth and stagger along the path, fighting to keep from crying out at the stab of each step. The fog circles my feet, billows up to my knees, my thighs, my waist, until I can't see the pot. But it's not fog—it's steam and smoke. I've reached the burning ground again. I stumble. It can't be much farther or I'll have to turn back. My skin is on fire. I cough, I gag, blinded by smoke.

Something brushes my face. I scream and almost drop the pot.

It is leaves, heart-shaped leaves.

I try to hold the pot in one arm, to have the other free to climb. But the pot is impossibly heavy. I could pitch it into the smoke and climb down the beanstalk fast. But what if it isn't waiting for me at the bottom?

I hold the half-circle handle with both hands and squint against the smoke. If only I wore a belt, I could buckle it through this handle.

It's a third hand I need.

I think of Flora balancing the laundry basket on her head. I try to lift the pot to my head but I cannot lift it higher than my mouth.

My mouth. I bite the handle and fear my lower jaw will crack as I climb down. The vine sears my palms. I climb so fast, I am falling from limb to limb. The handle cuts into my mouth. I half slide, half climb, faster and faster and faster—until I let go.

· · ·

"What have you done to yourself? Your poor mouth!" Mother presses sicklewort at the corners to staunch the bleeding. "And your feet are nothing but blisters." She clucks around me, dabbing with a cloth that reeks of balm. "What were you doing up there on the beanstalk?"

I work to form the single word: "Gold."

"Gold? What madness is this now? And what is this pot of stones?"

Stones? No! I try to push up to a sitting position. But my stomach wrenches. I roll to one side and spit out blood. Slowly I get on all fours. I look at the overturned pot. It is whole. Thank Heaven. I reach out and knock the pot aside.

A pile of stones.

The world goes black.

CHAPTER SIXTEEN

Flowers

Another month goes by.

I am setting stones in place on the path to the house I'm building. I look carefully to see where the next stone should go. My mind measures every detail.

Then I turn to my black pot. This is the same pot that the woman in the sky helped me hide behind the bush. The gold that once filled this pot seems unreal now, but I still hear her: "Take me away."

I pick out a stone, and it nestles into place. Just right.

I remember what Father taught me long ago, when we

built the irrigation ditches. I overlap certain stones, inter-lock others, moving with a certainty that isn't my own. The pot is always full. The size of the stones varies as the job varies. Every time I pick a stone, it fits perfectly. Sometimes I sense Father's hand leading mine as I reach in for the next stone.

I replaced the thatched roof of our cottage with the thinnest flat stones, arranged in overlapping layers. The mica sparkles in the sun. From the new wider rafters Mother hung strings of onions and apples, which perfume the air in a strangely pleasant way.

I repaired our barn with stones, too, and the wall be-side Flora's house, the one that runs along her laundry line. It's so sturdy, I can walk on it. I built a wall around our bean plants, which grow in the two fields we now own. I paid Ian Hedley a handsome purse in place of half the harvest to come, just so that we'd be clear of him. The bean plants stand tall and healthy within that wall. I built a stone chicken coop for our many chicks. The hen keeps laying and we keep selling eggs, but we bought a rooster from Flora's father and I set aside several nestfuls to come to term. Just last week they started hatching. As long as we can trade beans for feed, we can raise chickens year-round. That way we'll always have eggs and meat to sell. I like all these little chicks, their clucks. I've made them special water holes, special roosting shelves. Mother watches me and she smiles.

I know Mother is happy, even without her smiles. I know because of her flower garden. She stopped working it after Father died. After all, she worked all day for other farmers and sewed by candlelight all evening. There was no time for flowers. But last week she cleared away the brush and scrub. She wants me to build stone retaining walls, for a garden with different levels. I'll put steps from one to the next. We'll plan it together this winter. So these stones will keep me busy through the cold months, too.

But for now, I'm building this house. It has a large entrance room and two smaller rooms, just for sleeping. The entrance room has two chimneys, one opposite the other. The one on the south side is the cooking hearth. The other is for extra warmth. This makes it a finer home than most.

But it's the courtyard that makes this house special. The courtyard is three times the size of the entrance room, as large as the courtyards in the center of manor houses. It lies between the entrance room and the two rear sleeping rooms. I hadn't planned to make a courtyard. But when I was fitting stones into the roof of the entrance room, one was smooth at the edges, forming a perfect rim. It reminded me of the lip of a well, it was so clean. I ran my hand along that rim and I liked it. I could see the idea for the courtyard then. Maybe the idea was in the stones themselves.

I built a stairway from one corner of the courtyard up to the roof, where I fashioned a walkway around the top. It gives a view of the countryside in every direction.

Flora clears her throat. She's been standing behind me for several minutes. I knew it, of course. I smelled her sweetness. But I enjoy her eyes on my hands in this task. I enjoy knowing that she is still amazed at the way the stones come together as tightly as woven wool. She comes to my side. "Have you ever been out here, here at the house, at night, Jack? Have you sat in the courtyard and looked up in the deepest dark?" She makes the smallest laugh. "Walls all around and the heavens above. You must feel safe."

"At night the stars twinkle down to the dirt floor." I put another stone in place. "The moon tells stories."

Flora takes a pebble from my pot. It's black and round. "This is beautiful."

"Take it."

She puts it in her pocket and walks past me, through the doorway and the entrance room into the courtyard. She stands in the center and looks up. "In the day the sun warms it." Her voice is wistful. "What's it for, Jack? Who will use this courtyard?"

I tap my foot on the ground. "This dirt is not for beans. It's not for oats or wheat or barley."

"I could guess that." Her face stays pointing to the sky, her eyes closed now.

I feel a flash of silly happiness at being near her. But I'm never completely happy: two women cry in my head, one in the clouds, one here beside me. I take a stone from my pot. Flora looks back over her shoulder at me. Even at this distance her eyes search mine. I turn my head away and try to whistle, though it still hurts my jaw to pucker my lips.

"Tell me."

I put down the stone and join her in the center of the courtyard. I hadn't asked myself before what this courtyard is for. It didn't matter. My hands built it for its own sake. But the answer comes easily: "Pleasure." I look her in the eye.

"What do you mean?"

"This courtyard will be for dreaming. For thinking and breathing under sun and stars . . . and for . . ." I lean toward her.

She blushes and looks away.

"Pleasure," I say.

I almost laugh at myself: pleasure. Each day the beans need to be picked, the eggs need to be gathered and sold. And at the end of the day, I build. Work is my only pleasure.

"A room just for pleasure." Flora's voice is quiet. "Stonemasons have been coming here, to our county, you know."

"I didn't know." I haven't paid attention to the news in town.

"Oh, yes. They've brought knowledge of how stone houses are made elsewhere."

"Oh."

"They make them in France and lots of places. My grandfather lived in a stone house."

"I remember." My voice breaks on the words as I think of the house I once promised myself I'd build for Flora. But she seems not to notice.

"They withstand fire so much better, of course. Some are using not just stone, but brick from excavated Roman roads." She puts her palms together like sleeping birds. "Some of the stone manors have courtyards, too. But none of them has a walkway like yours. This will be the best house anywhere, Jack."

I repeat her words inside my head.

"It's almost finished. What will you build next?"

"I don't know."

She nods. "And, Jack, who . . ." She crosses her arms and hugs herself. "Who will live here?"

My throat thickens. I let Flora's question shimmer in the air. Finally, I whisper, "Birds."

"Birds? I love birds."

I know that.

"What if birds don't come?"

"They'll come," I say, realizing only now how Mother has inspired me. "I'll plant flowers to lure them. I'll call this courtyard the flower court."

"My name means 'flower' in Spanish."

I didn't know that—something so important and I didn't know. Ah: this is her courtyard.

Flora spins around. "The stones in the pot seem never ending."

I dare to take her hand. "Many things are without end, Flora."

She pulls away gently. Her fingers hide in the folds of her skirt. "I'm happy you and your mother . . . I'm happy for you, Jack."

I let my head fall back on my neck, looking to the sky. "You're planning to wed soon. Are you happy for yourself?"

Clap!

I jerk my head up. Flora has clapped her hands in front of my face.

"You feel superior, don't you?" Her eyes are large and sad, despite the anger in her voice. "Well, you aren't, Jack. You won't starve, that's true. But you're still you. You're still half mad."

"What do I do that is mad?"

"Just look, you're building a courtyard for pleasure when you aren't even rich."

My blood speeds. "You stand here and dream. You do, Flora, you. Why?"

"How do you know what I do?" Her hands form fists. She shakes them at me. "You don't know, Jack. You know nothing."

"I haven't heard you hum or sing today. You hold it inside now."

"You think that means something? It means nothing."

"They're your birds, Flora—those songs. They're your hopes."

"Birds? Hopes? You talk crazy. You're crazy. Your head is thick and dull. Like a cannonball, Jack. Always ready to explode."

"If you want to hear an explosion, Flora, put your ear to the moon."

"See? See what you say!"

And now my heart beats wildly. "I know you don't want to marry William."

"Don't say that!" Flora rushes from the house and through the grasses. I race along beside her. She stops. "Don't you ever say that. Don't you dare. Come next September, you'll be howling again. You'll be dashing yourself against the rocks at the cliff base. You do it every year!"

"I won't have to. The beanstalk is there. I can climb the cliff any time I want."

"That's just it. You want to climb it, Jack. I knew it.

You want to climb that beanstalk and risk your life for no reason."

"I wouldn't call a hen that lays countless eggs no reason. I wouldn't call a pot that holds countless stones no reason."

Flora shakes her head. "You can say whatever you want to your mother, Jack. You can pretend that things have turned out like you planned. But don't pretend with me. The hen was an accident. I'm sure of it. So was the pot of stones. You go up that cliff just so you can look down from where your father fell. It's stupid and dangerous and crazy."

"If I hadn't been afraid to climb higher, I could have caught up with him. Nothing bad would have happened."

"Don't be absurd, Jack. You couldn't have protected him. You've have both died."

"I should have tried. I should have died trying."

"That's the nine-year-old talking." Flora puts her hands on my cheeks. "I know, Jack. When Mama died, I wanted to, too. I begged her to have a baby, I wanted a little brother so badly. I begged her." Tears brim in her eyes. "But I didn't know what I asked of her. How could I?" Her hands press firm against my cheeks. "I forgave myself, Jack. I stopped thinking about it."

"I can't."

"Yes, you can. You don't give yourself a chance so long as climbing that cliff is all you want."

I put my hands over hers. "That's not all I want, Flora."

Flora steps backward, pulling her hands away. "My

whole life people have looked at me as a foreigner. If I marry a madman, what chance do I have? What chance will my children have? I need to be safe." She runs.

"You need to fly out the courtyard into the sky," I call. "You need that, too, Flora. You need that, too!"

I walk back to my path. The stones sit patient in the pot, each one ready to be set in place. But I don't have the will to work.

I put the heavy pot in the handcart and wheel it homeward.

Mother looks up at me from the table. She is making round pasties of potatoes, onions, beans, and eggs. They're my favorite. The savory filling fries in the pan as she fits the bottom crusts into the tins.

"It smells wonderful."

Mother smiles. "Roll the top crust for me, won't you, Jack?"

"Course, Mother." I pick up the rolling pin and set to work.

Mother tilts her head just a little. "You usually build till evening." She puts a large scoop of filling into each bottom crust. Then I place the tops on. We crimp the edges of top and bottom crusts together. Mother makes slits with the knife, shooting out from the centers like sunbeams, and slides the pasties into the oven.

I drop into a chair.

She turns to me. "Speak, Jack. What's bothering you?"

"Flora doesn't sing anymore, Mother."

"There's blessing enough in good food and a solid home."

"Still, you spend time planning your flower garden, Mother."

"Yes."

"That's what I want, Mother. Something more."

Mother puts her hand on mine.

CHAPTER SEVENTEEN

Traps

A week passes.

Today I dig a well. The house will have fresh water close at hand, so no one will have to trudge far. I'll line the sides of the well with curved smooth stones, like the stones that ring the opening of the flower courtyard. I'll build a thick wall around the top where people can sit and talk and make wishes. The water will be cool, even in summer. I dig easily. My arms have grown thick and strong from lugging stones. I hear horse hooves and turn to watch William ride up.

"Close to finished, Jack?"

I grip my shovel and go back to digging. William will get to whatever it is he wants in his own good time.

"This isn't the best spot for a house."

I think of how close the house is to our bean fields. I will work those fields for the rest of my life. How close it is to Flora's house. I will watch her visit her father for the rest of his life. How far it is from the road. I don't have to talk with anyone if I don't want to.

I think of the smooth-barked beech tree beside the house. And the creek only fifty yards back that burbles along in spring. And the swifts that have been investigating the eaves of the flower court, eaves I built specially wide to harbor nests.

This house is in the perfect spot.

"Go back to your mudhole, William."

William gets off his horse and clomps toward me. "Now listen here, Jack. I try to be civil and you act like a bloody rude fool all the time. Don't think I don't know why."

I dig.

William grabs the shovel from my hands and throws it aside. "Do you want to know why? You're consumed with jealousy. That's what it is. You harebrain. As if Flora would ever look at you."

"She thinks I'm the handsomest youth in the valley."

"Handsome? You're good for nothing."

"I built this house."

William turns a full circle in his frustration. He faces me again. "Listen, if you live here, you'll have to endure seeing Flora and me come visit her father year after year. You'll die of hate and envy."

I climb out of the well and look down it.

William grabs me by both shoulders and turns me to face him. "Let me help you, Jack. I'll trade houses with you. I just built a wonderful house, much better than this one. The oven is so big, you could roast a whole pig in it." His face is earnest.

"I don't eat pigs."

"Then roast a leg of mutton."

"I don't eat animals."

"Listen, I'll buy this house from you. You can take your mother and move to another county. South. Yes, you can set up a new life and build a new house. You'll even look sane, if you grow bean plants and build walls and paths and make yourself useful. You can find a woman suitable for you."

I knock his hands from my shoulders and step back.

"It's a generous offer. Don't be crazy. I'll pay you well."

"Why?"

"What does it matter why?"

And now I guess: "Flora wants to live here."

"Yes." William shakes his head ruefully. "She's got some silly notion that this house is special."

"Birds and hopes," I say.

"What?"

"I won't sell."

William squinches up his face in anger. "Don't be absurd. This is the house Flora wants. I'll pay what you ask."

I fetch my shovel, hop back in the hole, and dig.

"Are you deaf? Name your price."

I dig.

"Answer me! I've made a generous offer."

I look up at him. His face is purple with rage. I dig.

"I could have you driven off this land. It would be easy to convince people you were a menace. I could simply take the land."

"And what would Flora think of that?"

William's eyes almost pop from his head. "You drive me to say things I don't even mean, you miserable . . ." He pauses. "I wish you no harm, can't you see that?"

I dig.

He paces. "I'll have another house built. Exactly the same as this one. It'll be far away. I'll build a cottage for her father, too. And he'll live near us. And she'll never come this way again. You'll never see her again."

"And she'll never see me. That's what you really want, right? That's what you're afraid of: her seeing me."

"It doesn't matter how you say it—you'll never see each other. You're a jackass. That's your real name: Jack-Ass. When you come to your senses, let me know." William climbs on his horse and gallops away.

I drop the shovel. That is the man Flora will marry.

I can't bear them any longer, these traps, so many traps. Me and Flora. And the woman in the sky. We're all trapped.

The blight and the drought and the wagers gone wrong—they trapped Father, too. They made him forget his own words. He said we needed three things: food on the table and a roof over our heads and each other. It's the third one he forgot, the most important one. We needed each other. Losing Father hurt Mother and me so much more than anything else could have.

Oh! I see it now. One, two, three. Without three, what's the point?

I race for the beanstalk.

CHAPTER EIGHTEEN

The Final
Visit

I grab the axe from the woodpile, grip low on the handle, and hoist the head over my shoulder as I walk. The ground beneath my feet is hard with frost. Coneys hop on the hills. Crows caw.

Everything is normal except me. I carry an axe, whose blade I sharpened just yesterday. I walk ever faster toward the beanstalk.

But my eyes won't stay on the path. They wander back to the hills. I see a sheep, a ewe. I hear her bleat as she gives birth. I stop and watch the newborn lamb struggle to its feet. The ewe licks the lamb as it nurses. I walk on.

I drop to my knees before the beanstalk. I take the axe off my shoulder and look it up and down one more time. When I grabbed it from the woodpile, I was so sure. But now . . . My eyes follow the newborn lamb. I try to imagine the head of this axe biting in between the giant's shoulder blades, and I drop the axe and retch.

When I can stand again, my head clears, my body feels lighter. The giant in the sky is the monster—not me. I will manage with my wits, however limited they may be.

I pull a leaf from the beanstalk and chew. The sweet green liquid cleanses my mouth.

I climb.

The first time I climbed this beanstalk, the hen was a surprise. An accident, like Flora said. The hen that lays countless eggs—food on the table.

The second time, I expected magic. The pot of gold seemed almost to be waiting for me. The pot that gives countless stones—a roof over our heads.

What will it be this time? What will the third thing be? I climb faster.

I try to remember everything about my last two visits to the castle. I try to see what was in the big room, where everything lay. I must not be taken by surprise. And in a flash I realize something: the woman, the giant, the castle and all its contents—all of it is shades of gray, from almost white to almost black. A colorless world.

Is this another trick of the eyes?

I must rely on other senses.

Evening has fallen quickly and I see only poorly now

anyway. The air grows dark and cool. How can it be this cool when it was so hot last time? But it's more than a month later and it's night, of course—night on the cliff top should be frigid.

I climb. The fog enters my ears. My fingers go stiff with cold and my eyeballs sting.

I climb more slowly as the temperature plummets, for my knees can barely bend. I stop and try to catch my breath. The air jabs inside my chest, as though icicles form in my lungs.

I use all my strength to uncurl my fingers. It hurts so badly, but I have to. I put one foot out, then the other. And, oh, I'm standing in the fog.

I creep along the icy ground on all fours, and my palms freeze. I rise on my knees so that I can cross my arms at the chest and fold my hands into my armpits. Now I move forward on my knees alone. They slip, but not as badly as my feet would if I walked. It is cold, so cold, and it is impossible to know whether I'm going in the right direction. But I have to keep moving; if I stop, I am dead.

I get on my feet with stabbing pains and shuffle to keep from falling. The skin on my cheek is parchment; it would rip with the slightest wind. I tuck my head; my lips chap, my teeth chatter.

And now I am tired, so tired. I never should have stood up. If only my knees would warm enough to buckle, I could fall to the ground, stretch out. I could sleep on clouds. They'd make a blanket.

I want to stop. I have to stop. But still, I take another listless step. My eyes lower to the ground, a limitless bed.

Forever.

Alone.

"Jack? Jack, Jack, you came again. I knew you would, I knew, but I didn't dare hope it would be this soon." She is beside me now, her arms encircling me, her hot breath blessing me. "I've been waiting for you." She half carries me, shivering against her, through the piercing cold into the castle.

The heat of a hearth fire warms even the stones of the corridor. Every step is a prayer come true. I lean into her.

She holds me tight. "Jack, my poor man. My good man." She helps me up onto the giant's chair at the huge table. She cries now. "I'm so glad you're here." Scabs cover both arms; a bruise blackens her throat.

My teeth clench with anger now more than cold. "Where is he?"

"He goes off for hours without saying a word."

"How long has he been gone?"

"Just a little while. He won't come back soon."

"Good. I need time to rest. But I'll take you with me." I remember her hand stroking the giant's cheek as he lay sleeping the last time I left. "Will you come?"

"Yes, yes." She cries harder. "You won't be sorry. I'll do anything for you, Jack."

"You don't have to do anything. We'll climb down the beanstalk."

"What?"

"The beanstalk. It grows up the cliff."

"How could a beanstalk climb all the way up this cliff?" She pulls away and wipes her tears. "I've looked down before. It's so far down, we're above the clouds. And a beanstalk would be too thin to hold us anyway. I won't go on a beanstalk."

"Then we'll go the way you came. How did you get here?"

"The giant carried me over one shoulder as he jumped the divide. I was but a girl, the wife of a young robber." Her trembling hands smooth her hair. "The giant lured me with a gold necklace. A single strand of gold." She laughs sadly. "I married my husband for wealth and he turned out to be a bumbler as a robber. Then I came here with the giant for the beautiful things he gives me every day. I have a huge box of them. But what good are riches to a prisoner? He refuses to carry me back. And there's no other way to escape."

"I'll show you the way. It will work."

She twists her ring around and around her finger. Her hand stretches toward the table, set with a sumptuous meal. "Eat," she says softly.

A pungent sauce covers the meat so that I cannot recognize the flesh. My stomach growls. "I didn't come for food."

"You're not angry at me, are you?" She plucks at her bodice nervously.

"No."

"Wait. I'll fetch a blanket to warm you. We should go as soon as you're ready." She rushes from the room.

The instant she is gone, the table draws my eyes again. Shredded cabbage steams under melting butter. Tender baby carrots are piled high in a bowl. Tiny new peas mixed with whole pearl onions call to me. But we must fly.

The woman returns with a blanket. She wraps it around my shoulders. Then she rubs my feet in her hands. "They're still icy." Her tears come again as she continues to rub.

I teeter on the edge of the chair. Then I get to my feet. "What happened to the man who took the giant's beans?"

She looks confused.

"Seven years ago. What happened to him?"

"Oh, him." She looks down. "We ran to climb down the cliff, but the giant came." She stops, growing pale.

"And?"

She opens her hands in surrender. "The giant ate him."

"No!" I grab her by the upper arms and shake her. "You should have stopped him! I would have!"

"You've seen him. No one can stop him."

A hateful death, hateful beyond belief. But there's still a chance it wasn't Father. "Did you burn his clothes?"

She shakes her head. "I threw them over the side of the cliff."

I collapse in her arms and heave with sobs.

The woman helps me back to the chair. She cradles my head under her chin. "Did you know him?"

"I loved him."

She dries my eyes with a corner of the blanket. "I'm sorry," she whispers.

I look around. This is where Father died. Perhaps this very room. I can't stand the thought. Still, Father didn't 120 give himself to the clouds. For that I am grateful. And

Flora was right: I couldn't have protected him. "All for magic beans."

"Black beans," the woman says. "Ordinary."

Now I look into her ashen eyes. "Why is everything here shades of gray?"

"Not just gray; gold, too. It's a curse. The giant came upon a stash of jewels in a cave at the bottom of a hill. He knew it was a fairy larder, but in his greed, he plundered it. Stupid giant. The fairy queen punished him by banishing all colors from this home except gold—to remind him of why he's been cursed." The woman looks around. "I hate all this gray. But the giant doesn't care. He says gold is all that matters anyway. You believe that too, don't you? Isn't that why you came here in the first place?"

No, I am thinking. I saw the colors of the rainbow the last time I came here. I believe in more than gold.

The ground shakes.

Then: "Fee!"

"No!" she cries.

"Fi!"

"Hide, Jack." She runs and opens the oven door.

I grab the carving knife. Then I drop it, like I dropped the axe.

"Fo!"

"Please, Jack." She sobs. "Please."

The chair! I could try to fend him off with it. But I can't lift it.

The castle door bangs open. "Fum!"

I run and jump into the oven. The door closes behind me.

"I smell the blood of an Englishman." Steps crash along the corridor. "Be he live or be he dead, I'll grind his bones to make my bread." He stamps around the room. "Where is he?" he shouts.

Her feet patter. "My sweet, my precious, you're so early. I didn't expect you back till dark."

Crash. Clatter.

"Now look what you've done. The oat barrel is ruined."

"It teased me, like the bread bowl. Like you!" *Slap.* The oven shakes.

This oven roasted my father. It will not roast me.

"I slaved all afternoon to cook for you," she says.

"You slave to keep yourself alive."

She whimpers. "You know I work to please you."

"You've hidden him."

Crack. She screams.

I push against the oven door, ready to charge, but something presses back. I cannot move it.

"I smell blood."

"The blood of the lamb."

"Hmmm. Nothing's been eaten yet."

"I was waiting for you."

"Good. Eat with me now." His voice is gruff, but changed now, as though he's trying to be affectionate. "Come and eat."

"I'll try."

"Are you sure nothing is stolen?"

"I'm sure."

"You've made two mistakes already." He snorts.

"Let's eat." At last he says, "Come here. I brought you a gift."

"Let me see. Ah. They go perfectly with the necklace, don't you think so?"

"Anything looks perfect on you. Kiss me."

"Wouldn't you like to hear the lyre?" she asks.

"Not now."

"Please. It would do us both good. We need it. Please."

"Fetch it, then."

She walks slowly. Her feet seem to drag. She returns. "Play!"

A filigree of notes seeps around the oven door, fills every hole, echoes in my head. The urgency within me eases. This music is the mystery of fog and fairies in the moors. It is the promise of rainbows in the brilliant sunlight. This is the incantation of the gods. The woman is a master.

"Come to me," he says. "Sit on my lap. Wrap your arms around me."

The music continues. How? It's impossible for her to play and wrap her arms around him at the same time. Yet the music never falters.

Small growly noises. Clever woman—she has mesmerized the monster with her music. The thunder snore comes now. The music stops.

I press on the oven door. This time it opens.

He sleeps in the chair, his head lolling to one side. She sits in his lap, locked against his chest by those massive arms. She doesn't look at me, but the rigidness of her neck tells me she's awake.

The lyre stands on the floor, several feet from the giant. I look at it, uncomprehending. It is there, but she is in the giant's lap.

The lyre must make music on its own.

I look back at the woman. How to free her? I make a step toward her.

"Stay there," she hisses, her head still turned away from me. "I can manage on my own. And you might wake him."

She peels his fingers loose, places one of his hands on his knee and holds the other one, then slips under that arm and off his lap. I can see her face now. Blood on her swollen nose.

"Hurry," I whisper.

"No. My jewelry." She tiptoes out of the room.

The giant snorts in his sleep. He tosses his head.

My heart jumps.

His snores come evenly spaced again.

She appears, pulling a large box by a rope.

I rush to her. "Are you mad? We must run."

"This is my treasure."

"You can't carry that down the beanstalk."

"But you can. You carried the pot of gold. We'll be rich."

"Leave that box and maybe we'll get away alive."

"Don't be a fool, Jack. Take. There's more gold in his pocket."

In his pocket? Has she completely lost her mind? The box scrapes as she drags it behind her. The giant sighs in his sleep.

"Don't go empty-handed, Jack. Take the lyre, at least."

The lyre. The lyre that gives so much pleasure. This must be the third thing. I tuck it under my arm and tiptoe ahead.

"Wake, Master. The thief leaves."

The giant's eyes pop open. He blinks.

I look quickly at the woman, shocked by the betrayal. She returns my terrified look.

"Hurry, Master!" comes the harmonious voice.

It is the lyre that betrays me!

The giant jumps to his feet.

"Run!" I scream. I am already at the door to the long corridor.

The giant grabs me by one arm and flings me across the room. Then he stomps toward the woman. "Traitor!"

I stagger to my feet as the giant lifts the jewel box over his head and brings it down with a crushing blow on the woman's head. She falls, lifeless.

In horror I jump out the window. I dash for the beanstalk. The monster crashes behind me. I run into the fog. The lyre calls out, a trail through fog. I hug it tight, but it calls out more loudly.

I slip and fall. The ground is ice again. I get to my feet and half run, half slide, one hand stretched out in front, feeling my way.

The giant falls behind me and the ground bounces. But now he's running again.

The air freezes my face, my chest. I slide. 125

He gains on me.

How much farther? The tears on my cheeks are ice. At last my hand touches the beanstalk. My fingers are so stiff, they can hardly close around it. I push one arm through the strings of the lyre, so that it hangs from my shoulder, and close my other hand on the stalk.

The giant grabs me around the waist in a bear swipe. He presses me to him with both arms. I kick, scratch, thrash. He squeezes. I scream as a rib snaps.

I pull the lyre off my shoulder and hold it out at arm's length over the beanstalk. "I'll drop it," I croak out with my last breath.

He reaches toward the lyre. As he moves, I twist sideways and with all the force of my life I bite the arm that holds me. He howls and lets go.

I fall, holding the lyre fast in one hand, gasping for breath. My other hand reaches out frantically into the void. Ah! I'm caught. I dangle by a knee on a leaf stem, upside down. The giant descends from above. Leaf stems crack under his weight. I grab the beanstalk with my free hand and right myself. I thrust my arm through the lyre strings again, pull it up to my shoulder, and climb down.

The whole beanstalk shakes from the giant. Leaves fall on my head.

I descend faster, faster. I would jump, but the lyre might crack apart.

The giant is only a few feet above me.

I half slide from leaf stem to leaf stem, faster and faster.

My feet hit the ground. I lay the lyre down, careful but swift, grab the axe, and swing. The beanstalk is strong as hardwood. I chop.

His grunts are louder, closer.

I chop. Please, beanstalk. Please.

He's coming.

I swing the axe.

The beanstalk teeters as the axe cuts through.

He screams.

Everything crashes around me.

CHAPTER NINETEEN

Treasure

It is mid-December, but not near cold yet.

I sit in the flower courtyard under the dimmest light of the moon in clouds, and I play the lyre.

I play a freedom song for the woman of the castle, who sways in my memory.

I play a funeral dirge for the giant, who lies buried at the foot of the cliff. I dug the grave myself. The body shrank to the size of an ordinary man as it hit the ground. It was battered beyond recognition. It could have been the body of any man, any poor enchanted soul finally freed from a hideous spell.

The huge beanstalk shriveled as well. I laid it in a coil on top of the body. Then I covered all with dirt and marked the grave with stones.

I play a song of parting, at long last, for Father and me. The music carries my tears and my love.

I told no one the tale.

Father's climb up the cliff has led where it would.

Now that tale is done; but mine goes on.

I play my story in a harvest chant for the bushels and bushels of beans that our fields produced all through the autumn. Winter will be upon us soon, so Mother and I can finally rest. The profits of that harvest will carry us easily to next spring. Mother won't take in sewing ever again. She loves it that we have set aside many beans for a spring planting. There will be more abundant harvests next year and the year after that, and on and on. The beanstalk did its job well.

It is me who plays this music, not the lyre itself. When I brought the lyre home, it sat silent. I knew that would happen, of course. But when I made my first tentative pluck at the strings, I was overjoyed to find that the tone of the lyre remained divine. I plucked every string. I sat with Mother at the table and together we listened as the majestic notes filled the room.

This month I have practiced every day. My fingers have become disciplined, and my ear, acute. I began by mimicking the sound of a stream, the wind around the eaves. I played fire crackling and mice scurrying. Finally

I mimicked the birdcalls. Mother said my musical talent comes from Father.

I play now a wedding march for Flora and William, who will walk the aisle tomorrow. But, oh, the night has passed already; dawn edges rosy over the horizon.

I lay the lyre on the ground and breathe hot on my fingers. I hang my heart on the last ring of the last note. I get on my knees and kiss the stone floor. "Today," I say to the floor and the walls, "today I give you away. You will be my wedding gift to Flora."

I hear a gasp.

Flora comes into the room, holding a tin box. "You're giving me this house?"

"I built it for you." For a while I tried to convince myself I could bear to live here without her. But I'm past such pretenses. "Anyway, I can't stand the idea of you living in the house William built. A house with a huge oven."

"What do you mean?"

"It doesn't matter."

She shakes her head. I cannot see her expression with her face turned like that. I sit again and look up at the open sky. Flora sits beside me.

We watch the clouds move. A wind rises.

Flora moves closer.

I sense her pulse, her lips, her sweet heat in the cool morning. I dare to put my arm around her. She doesn't raise her face to mine, but her shoulders yield themselves to me. With my other hand, I take hers. Our fingers interlace. "How long have you been here?"

"All night. Listening."

"A night together at last." I rub the cold from my arms and legs. "It isn't what I'd have imagined."

She laughs. "It's starting to rain. Shall we go under a roof?"

"Not me." I turn my face up and open my mouth. The rain tastes wonderful.

"Not enough sense to get out of the rain, Jack, oh, Crazy Jack." Her voice teases me.

I laugh now. "And this is how you spent the last night before your wedding. Sensible Flora."

Flora grows serious. "I'm not so sensible, it seems."

"And I'm not crazy anymore, Flora."

She looks at me.

"So, tell me, why did you come?"

She gives a little laugh and reaches for the tin box beside her. She hands it to me.

Inside is a jumble of rocks and feathers and bits of wood and dirty ribbon, all with oat seeds scattered through. I take out one of the brighter feathers.

"A scarlet tanager," says Flora. "You gave me that only two months ago." She reaches into the box and takes out a handful of feathers. "And this is a jay. You gave it to me three years ago. And this is a waxwing from one year ago. And this finch is from ten years ago. And . . ." She drops the feathers back in the box. "I saved everything you gave me. Everything ever. I was going to give it all back last night."

"And now?"

Flora flushes. She closes the box and looks around. She runs her fingers along the lyre's strings. "You play beautifully." 131

"The lyre is magnificent. No one can play poorly with that lyre."

"It was you, Jack. I love how you played." She hands me the lyre as she talks. "Will you play again now? Something just for me?"

I sit and play. Not the songs everyone knows, no. I play Flora's private hum. I play her lilting singsongs. I play her soft, laughing jingles. And as I play, the sun rises.

A rainbow forms. Violet, indigo, blue, green, yellow, orange, red. I stop playing and watch the colors of the sky. They enter through my eyes, they penetrate my bones.

A swift alights on the edge of the roof opening.

"He's listening." Flora moves close to me. She whispers, "I recognized some of the songs, but not all."

I smile at her. "Then you recognize only part of yourself."

She moves closer still. "Do you really know me that well, Jack?"

"Sometimes I think I know your heart, Flora."

Tears well in her eyes. "Help me, Jack," she whispers. "Help me know all of me."

And so I am playing again. I play hesitantly at first. I play her feet, the way her toes curl now in the sunshine. I play the tight bun of her hair and the strands that have sprung loose in the drizzle. I go around and around, my confidence growing.

Now I dare to play the flight of her hands when she's
happy. And she hums along, her hands swooping and

soaring. I play her eyes. She rises and dances. I play her strong dancing heart, her brown dancing body. I play her lips.

And she is crying.

I lay down the lyre.

She sits and nestles under my arm. "Oh, Jack, you make me believe in pleasures I put aside. Childish pleasures."

"What pleasures, Flora?" I run my hand along her arm. "Did you put aside loving?"

"Don't make me sound so cold."

"I didn't mean it that way," I whisper.

"Life was harsh after so many deaths."

"We're alive, Flora."

"And you grew crazy. My own Jack. Mad."

"Not really mad."

"Oh, yes. You were. You grew crazy. So I grew up. Or I thought . . . that was growing up." She pulls away and sits facing me. "Jack, tell me your heart."

"You know it, Flora."

"I do." She puts her hand to her mouth.

"Trust me. Trust your Jack."

"Jack, oh, Jack, what will happen next September? On the anniversary of his death. What will you do?"

"The beanstalk shriveled up, Flora. I buried it, and with it I laid to rest the past. I will never go back to the cliff."

"Never?"

"I speak the truth with you. I always have. My head is clear now and my heart . . . it's full of you."

Flora knits her brows. "But William, poor William."

"He'd be worse off if you married him when you love me."

She stands and pulls me to my feet. "It's early, Jack. There's time to make it right."

Time at last to make everything right. To have food on the table and a roof over our heads, but most of all, to have each other.

I take Flora into my arms, warm and good.